VENGEANCE

WHEN A LOVED ONE IS HARMED AND THE
SYSTEM LETS YOU DOWN, WHAT WOULD
YOU DO?

MARK DAVID ABBOTT

.

MARK DAVID ABBOTT

For K.
Thank you

JOIN MY NEWSLETTER

The next book is currently being written, but if you sign up for my VIP newsletter I will let you know as soon as the next book is released.

By signing up for the newsletter you will also receive advanced discounted links to all new-releases.

Your email will be kept 100% private and you can unsubscribe at any time.

If you are interested, please visit my website

www.markdavidabbott.com
(No Spam. Ever.)

PROLOGUE

John pulled her in close, and she rested her head on his shoulder as they gazed out across the valley. The sun was low on the horizon, the evening light transforming the hills of the Western Ghats into silhouettes of blue and grey. Far below, a peacock called as the smell of woodsmoke from village cooking fires was carried to them on a gentle breeze.

"Isn't it heavenly?" Charlotte turned and smiled up at John.

John gazed down at her—the crinkles around the corners of her blue eyes, the curl of blond hair falling down across her sun-kissed forehead. He smiled, squeezing her tighter and planted a kiss on her forehead as she snuggled in close.

"I'm so glad we moved here," she sighed.

"Me too."

They stood in silence for a moment, content in each other's company, until a growl from John's stomach interrupted their thoughts.

"Come, let's go and get something to eat. I'm famished."

"Wait." Charlotte broke free and pulled her phone from the back pocket of her jeans. "I want to capture this."

John waited as she took a photo, then, hand in hand, they walked back downhill to the homestay.

John was one year into a two-year posting to India, and he didn't think it was going to be long enough. Every weekend and public holiday, he and Charlotte took off from Bangalore to explore the country, but there was still so much to see and do. They had visited the well-known tourist destinations in the first few months—the Taj Mahal, Rajasthan, Bodh Gaya—but were now content to visit lesser known, less touristy spots. This weekend, John had taken an extra day off, and they had made the five-hour drive from Bangalore to the little town of Ooty. A hill station in the Western Ghats, it was blessed with beautiful scenery and a cool climate perfectly suited for growing tea. The daylight hours were spent exploring, long walks through the tea plantations, occasionally stopping to watch the Tamilian women plucking the tender green tea leaves and dropping them in the baskets slung over their backs, their brightly colored saris, gold jewelry, and shy smiles standing out in stark contrast against the emerald green tea bushes. Charlotte thought of them as human butterflies flitting across the landscape. The evenings were enjoyed in the homestead relaxing in front of a fire, sharing whiskey with the owner, a third-generation planter, while he regaled them with stories of life on the estate. Tales of man-eating tigers, elephant incursions, leopards stealing dogs, and the constant labor issues inherent amongst the itinerant tea picking workforce. It was fascinating and a lifestyle they couldn't even imagine when back home in England.

John and Charlotte had been married for two years now and were still as much in love as the days before they were married. When the offer came from the bank that employed John to go and manage their back-office operations in Bangalore, they had jumped at the opportunity for adventure. The chance to escape the routine and dull weather of England for the exotic land of India, a land John had only read about in the books of Kipling and Corbett, was too good to pass up.

It was everything they expected it to be and more—exciting, exotic, chaotic, frustrating, and exasperating, but never boring. They both thought they would never be able to go back to a normal life in England ever again.

As John and Charlotte neared the homestead, the owner's pair of Labradors bounded up to them, jumping and wagging their tails in delight as if seeing them for the first time. The cook waved to them from the door of the kitchen, and John's mouth watered at the smell of exotic herbs and spices cooking away.

"I wonder what we will have tonight?"

"Whatever it is, it smells fantastic. Indian food in England is nothing like this. I don't think I can ever eat in an Indian restaurant back home again!"

John chuckled. "I don't think I will be happy with food anywhere else ever again." He kicked off his walking shoes outside their room and pushed open the door. "Let's freshen up and go and sit in the lounge. I want to hear a few more of Deepak's stories."

Charlotte laughed and punched him in the arm.

"Yeah, right. You just want to help him finish the whiskey bottle you both started on last night."

Beeeeep!

John banged the heel of his hand on the horn as the car beside him moved across into his lane. The driver moved back, but ten seconds later moved across again. John slammed his palm on the horn again, braked to let the car pull in and shook his head. He had only been back in Bangalore two days but already missed the quieter roads of Ooty.

The drive home from John's office in the Manyata Tech Park on the northern edge of Bangalore was short in distance but fraught with potential danger. The roads were chaotic, vehicles of all shapes and sizes milling amongst each other with no sense of order and a complete disregard for personal safety. Added to that were the additional hazards of potholes, suicidal jaywalkers, and in scenes repeated in cities all over India—cows standing serenely in the middle of the traffic, chewing their cud as thousands of two and four-wheeled vehicles swarmed around them, like a four-legged Moses parting the Red Sea. The local driving habits still confounded him even after a year in the country.

Rules, road markings, and traffic signals served only as suggestions to be ignored by the majority of the driving public. Most expats and indeed many Indians chose to employ a driver rather than drive themselves. However, John loved driving—even in these conditions—and didn't want to give up the driving seat to someone whose abilities he didn't fully trust. It had taken him a while to get used to it, and it was only when he decided to let go of all the things he thought were supposed to happen, the way things were "supposed" to run, he could drive with a certain element of ease. No point in trying to change everyone else. What was the expression? When in Rome...

John indicated right—one of the few vehicles to do so, indicators and side mirrors redundant for most drivers—and turned off the outer ring road onto Bellary Road which led north from the city toward the airport. Ahead, three men squeezed together on a single motorbike, swerved to avoid a crater-sized pothole, and he braked hard, flicking the steering wheel to the right to drive around them. Horns blared behind him, and he grinned. Perhaps he had become a local.

The road led straight for the next five kilometers, passing the Colombia Asia Hospital on the right, then the sprawling grounds of the Government Agricultural University on the left. This locality had once been at the extreme outskirts of the city, accessed by a single lane road, but Bangalore had expanded so rapidly, the area had been swallowed up and was now served by a six-lane highway.

Approaching a junction, he reduced his speed and checked for oncoming traffic, then turned across three lanes and into the access road which led to the gated housing estate he called home. He slowed for the entrance. The security guard, recognizing his vehicle, raised a hand in greeting and opened the gate. John drove through, thanking the guard with a wave and a smile, and cruised down the interior roadway past the rows of bungalows. It was still light, and a group of children played cricket in the street while others rode up and down on bicycles. At the sound of the approaching car, they stopped playing and moved to the side, resuming immediately after it had passed. John took the first left and then right, finally turning into the carport of his house.

Grabbing his briefcase from the seat beside him, he climbed out, pressing the key fob to lock the door behind him. He glanced across at the small front garden, at the lawn turning brown in the relentless sun, and made a mental note to remind the gardener to water it.

The front door opened just as he reached for the handle, and he paused to look at Charlotte, standing on the top step. Her cheeks were smudged with paint, and her blonde hair was piled up on top of her head in a small bun, exposing her long slim neck. Her beauty still took his breath away, even dressed in jeans and an old work-shirt.

She smiled, her eyes sparkling, "How was your day?"

Dropping the briefcase on the step, John wrapped his arms around her before kissing her on the lips.

He angled his head back to look down at her, not letting her go, "Nothing special today, baby. How was yours?"

Charlotte smiled up at him, "Great. I played tennis in the morning with Shalini but stayed home the rest of the day working on my paintings. I've almost finished the landscape. Come and take a look."

John slipped off his shoes at the door, a habit he had picked up in the last year and allowed himself to be led by the hand down the corridor and up the stairs to the spare bedroom which John had converted into a studio. Spare canvases on stretcher frames leaned against the side wall, and in one corner, a shelf unit was filled with brushes and paints. In the center of the room with its back to him was a large canvas on an easel, angled to make the most of the natural light streaming in from the large picture window. John stepped around it to take a look at the watercolor painting of the stunning hill range Charlotte had photographed during their weekend trip to Ooty.

"Wow, it looks fantastic."

Charlotte crossed her arms and cocked her head to one side as she cast a critical eye over her work.

"I still have a few things to finish, but it's almost done."

"It looks great. I knew there was a reason I married you instead of your sister."

Charlotte punched his upper arm and giggled, "Cheeky sod."

"You should really think about exhibiting your paintings, let other people see them and appreciate them."

"That's not why I do it. I paint because I love to paint. It makes me feel happy. I love it when I can transfer the images in my head to the canvas. I'm creating something from nothing."

John moved behind her, wrapping his arms around her, nuzzling her neck as they both looked at the painting.

"I know, Charlie, I'm just so proud of you and would love other people to see how talented you are."

He slipped his hand beneath her shirt and ran his fingers up her belly toward her breasts. Charlotte sighed and leaned back into him as he kissed her earlobe, then reluctantly pushed his hand away.

"Hey, not now." She giggled, "Go and get changed, Rohan and Shalini are coming around for a drink soon, and I need to get out of these painting clothes."

"Let me help you."

"Nooo, if you help me, we will never be ready when they arrive."

John admired her long denim-clad legs as she walked away toward the master bedroom to get changed. Every day, his love for her deepened. He thought back to the day when he first saw her in a cafe in Winchester. When she walked in, he thought she was the most beautiful woman he had ever seen, and he knew at that moment he would marry her. She sat at the next table, and after he summoned the courage to strike up a conversation, they hit it off immediately, getting married six months later after a whirlwind courtship that left both of them breathless and excited about the future.

"Do you need Sanjay tomorrow?" Charlotte called out to him from the en suite bathroom where she was already in the shower.

John walked into the bathroom and rested his butt against the vanity unit. His company paid for a driver, but as John preferred to drive himself, Sanjay drove Charlotte around most of the time. John didn't feel comfortable leaving Charlotte on her own on the roads. If anything happened or the car broke down, it was always better to have a local handle it.

"No, why?" he watched the water run down over her back.

"I'm attending an exhibition in the afternoon, then meeting Susan for dinner. I'll be back a bit late."

"No problem. I'll work later tomorrow then, I've got a report for head office I need to finish, anyway."

Charlotte turned to face him, and he felt a familiar stirring in his loins as he ran his eyes over her body, tanned and lithe from daily tennis, water running in rivulets down her flat belly.

Charlotte grinned at him, recognizing the look in his eyes and shook her head. "We don't have time."

As if in confirmation, they heard the sound of the doorbell.

"See, they are here already. I'll be down in a minute."

John pretended to scowl and went to open the door.

"Sanjay, drop me off at the front here."

"Yes, Madam," Sanjay replied before indicating right and pulling off Vittal Mallya Road into the Porte Cochere of U.B. City, a large luxury mall development in central Bangalore. He stopped outside the front entrance, and Charlotte reached into her purse, pulling out a one hundred rupee note and passed it toward Sanjay in the front seat.

"Get yourself something to eat, Sanjay, I will be awhile. I'll call you when I'm done."

Sanjay bobbed his head, "Yes Madam, thank you, Madam."

"Keep your phone on, Sanjay, remember what happened last time when your battery went flat, and I couldn't reach you."

"Yes, Madam, today it's fully charged. Call me anytime Madam."

Charlotte opened the door and stepped out of the car. Sanjay was a good driver and always helpful, but he had a bad habit of leaving his phone off or letting it run flat. The last time she had to hunt through the entire parking building before she found him sleeping in the car, his phone dead on the dashboard. Sanjay had an easy job, they didn't use him every day, but his young wife had recently had another baby, and Sanjay was more than a little sleep deprived, catching up on his sleep in the car whenever he could.

Charlotte walked through the metal detector in the mall entrance and passed her handbag to the female security guard for checking. The guard had a cursory look inside and waved her on with a smile. Charlotte couldn't figure out what purpose the guards served, their security checks were rudimentary at the best of times.

Susan was standing inside, scrolling through her phone, and looked up when Charlotte called out her name. They air-kissed each other and walked toward the escalators which led up to the restaurant level.

Susan was also English, and she and her husband Barry had been posted in Bangalore for three years now. She was considered an "old hand" and knew the city's restaurants and boutiques intimately. Susan had proven to be particularly helpful and a useful contact when Charlotte and John first moved to the city. They had become firm friends.

"How have you been, Charlotte?"

"Great, great. I've just come from the exhibition at Chitrakala Parishath."

"Oh yes, I've been meaning to go. How was it?"

"Quite interesting. Lots of works by local artists."

They reached the top of the escalator and walked out onto the podium before turning right toward the restaurants.

"You know Charlotte, you should really exhibit some of

your paintings. You are easily as good as most of these artists. I will be happy to help organize it for you."

"I don't know, Susan. John has been pushing me too, but I'm not sure it's what I want to do."

"Well, if you change your mind, let me know, I can get a lot of the expat wives to come along," said Susan, as they reached their favorite Italian restaurant and told the waitress at the entrance, "Two people, please."

The waitress led them to an empty table and handed them the menus.

"Now, tell me about your Ooty trip."

I t was almost eight pm by the time John reached home. It had been a long day filled with meetings, and later in the day when the time zones were suitable, confer-ence calls with his head office in London. John didn't usually like to work so late, but as Charlotte wasn't home, he had decided to catch up on some long pending work.

He dropped his keys on the kitchen counter and removed a cold bottle of Kingfisher from the fridge. As he closed the door, he noticed a note from Charlotte written on a yellow Post-it.

Honey, there is a pot of chicken curry on the stove and rice in the rice cooker. Enjoy, and I will call you when I leave. Lots of love. C. XXX

John looked at the pot on the stove and lifted the lid. Ah, that smells delicious! Replacing the lid, he took a swig from the beer bottle and walked upstairs to freshen up.

Later, showered and changed, he put a couple of spoons of rice onto a plate and ladled the steaming hot chicken curry over the rice. After removing another cold beer from the fridge, he took his plate into the lounge and sat on the sofa in front of the TV. He didn't expect Charlotte to be back until late, so he planned to catch up on a bit of sport. As much as he loved her, she didn't share his taste for the sporting channels, and it wasn't often he got time alone to watch a few games. It was cricket season in India, and there was a game on almost every night. Although he had never been a fan of cricket until he moved here, it was such a passion in the country, he couldn't help taking an interest in the game. If nothing else, it gave him something in common to discuss with his colleagues in the office.

The phone vibrating on the sofa beside him woke him sometime later. It took a few seconds for him to orientate himself, the TV was still on, and his empty plate lay on his lap. There was a damp patch on his shirt where he had dribbled. He must have dozed off while watching the game. He glanced at his watch, eleven-fifteen. He picked up his phone and checked the message.

Leaving now. See you soon.

John picked up his plate and moved to the kitchen. There wasn't much traffic at that time of night, so Charlotte should be home by midnight. Just enough time for him to wash up and grab another beer.

4

Charlotte put her phone away and waited for Susan to finish calling her driver. They were standing just outside the entrance to the shopping mall with other customers waiting for their drivers. Thankfully, Sanjay's phone had still been on, and he had promised Charlotte he would be there in a minute.

"Thank you, Charlotte, for a lovely dinner. It's always great to catch up with you."

Charlotte smiled, "I enjoyed it too. We must do it again soon. Give my love to Barry. I've not seen him for ages."

Susan sighed, "No, he's been traveling a lot to Delhi recently. It's all to do with getting the Government permits for the new factory his company is opening. You know how it is. You have to keep going higher up the chain of command until you can find someone who will clear the necessary documents without demanding a bribe. It's been a stressful time for him."

"Yes, I'm sure. Well, when he is in town next and has some time, let's all catch up for a meal. John would love to see him again too. Ah here's Sanjay."

Sanjay pulled up in the white Toyota Corolla and jumped out to open the rear door.

"See you soon, Susan," Charlotte and Susan hugged and air-kissed as Susan's car pulled up behind the Toyota.

"Yes, take care. My car has come too. Good night."

Charlotte waved goodbye, then sat in the back seat, thanking Sanjay as he closed the door behind her.

He ran around to the driver's side and climbed in.

"Have you eaten Sanjay?"

"Yes, Madam, thank you, Madam," he replied bobbing his head, his eyes smiling at her in the rear-view mirror.

"What did you have?" Charlotte asked, knowing full well that Sanjay often didn't buy a meal with the money she gave him but saved it and gave it to his wife when he got home.

"Curry and rice, Madam." Sanjay put the car in gear and pulled straight out onto the main road without looking, inviting a chorus of horns.

Charlotte winced and said a small prayer to herself before asking, "Was it good?"

"Yes, Madam. A little spicy but good."

"Okay, Sanjay, home please."

Sanjay bobbed his head from side to side and drove on up the road.

Charlotte sat back and closed her eyes, the late hour, half a bottle of red wine and a full stomach making her drowsy. It would take about forty minutes to reach home, so she might as well have a nap.

She was jolted awake as the car swerved suddenly. "Sorry, Madam. It was a big pothole. Hard to see in the dark."

"It's okay." Charlotte looked out the window. They were

just passing the Windsor Manor Hotel on the right and heading north toward Shivnagar, the favored suburb of many politicians and businessmen. Cauvery Theatre passed on the left, and Sanjay slowed for the Shivnagar junction before turning right and heading up the hill past Palace Grounds.

The interior of the car was lit up from behind as a car flashed its lights repeatedly, and Charlotte looked over her shoulder to see a car approaching at high speed. It pulled out to pass, horn blaring and lights flashing, a silver Audi A6 with blacked-out windows. It swerved across in front of the Toyota, but not before it had completely passed, the rear bumper scraping along the front corner of the Toyota. Sanjay braked hard, hitting the horn at the same time, cursing under his breath, and Charlotte was thrown forward against the front seat. The Audi skidded to a stop further up the road, its brake lights glaring malevolently in the darkness as Sanjay pulled to a complete stop.

"What a crazy driver!" Charlotte exclaimed, retrieving her handbag from the footwell and sitting back against the seat.

"I think drunk, Madam," Sanjay said and opened his door. "Please, wait inside. I will check the car."

He got out and walked toward the front of the car.

Charlotte watched Sanjay run his hand along the front of the bumper as she pulled her phone from her handbag and dialed John's number.

He answered on the third ring, "Hello."

"Some idiot driver just ran into us beside Palace Grounds."

"Oh my God, are you ok?"

"Yes, but I think the car is scratched. The other driver

must be drunk, he was driving so fast and swerved toward us. Completely his fault. Sanjay is just checking the car."

Charlotte looked out the front window where Sanjay was now bent over inspecting the damage. The driver of the Audi had got out and was walking toward him, shouting and waving his arms about. Sanjay straightened up and shouted back.

"Sanjay and the other driver are having an argument now."

"Well, don't worry, as long as you are okay. There is no point in getting into an argument with these guys. They will never pay up, and we are insured, anyway."

"Yes, you are right," agreed Charlotte.

The Audi's passenger doors opened, and three men climbed out and approached Sanjay and the driver who were still arguing. "Now three other guys have got out of the car."

"Tell Sanjay not to worry," said John. "It's better you get home safely."

Charlotte gasped as she saw the driver push Sanjay in the chest while the three passengers laughed. Sanjay protested, and the driver backhanded him across the face, sending him staggering backward. The three other men surrounded him and started pushing him back and forth.

"Oh, shit!" Charlotte cried out.

"What's happening, what's happening?"

"They are hitting Sanjay!"

"Tell him to get back in the car! And lock your doors!"

Charlotte pressed the switch to wind down her window, but the engine was turned off. She opened the door, put one foot out and cried out, "Leave him alone! Sanjay get back in the car!"

The men turned to the car, noticing her for the first time. They exchanged a glance, and the driver grinned. He said something to two of the men, and they started moving toward the car while he and the other man turned their attention back to Sanjay. The driver pushed Sanjay down onto the ground, then kicked him hard in the stomach. Sanjay cried out in pain and curled up, knees against his chest to protect his stomach. The other man started kicking him in the back.

Charlotte screamed and tried to close and lock the door. She wasn't fast enough, and her phone fell to the floor as the door was wrenched open and one of the men reached inside, grabbing her by the arm and pulled her out.

She struggled to get free, and he slapped her across the face with his free hand. Her cheek stung with the blow, and her eyes welled up with tears.

"Leave us alone!"

She could hear Sanjay's cries as the two men kicked him repeatedly, grunting with the effort. A car honked as it went by, slowing to see what was happening, but then promptly sped off. No-one would help for fear of being hurt themselves. They were on their own. She looked up at her attacker as he leaned over her, her arms pinned to the side of the car. His eyes were red, and she could smell alcohol on his breath as he looked her up and down. The other man joined him, swaying, unsteady on his feet but his eyes hungry with lust. He licked his lips and reached forward to touch her breasts. She tried to shift out of the way but couldn't move.

"Please leave us alone. I'll give you money."

They both laughed. "We don't need your money," he sneered. "But you will do nicely."

"Charlotte, Charlotte!" John screamed down the phone. He could hear voices in the background but couldn't make out what they were saying. "Charlotte!"

His hands were shaking, his heart pounding in his chest. He shouted down the phone, but there was still no response. He ended the call and dialed her number again. It rang and rang. He tried again and again, but there was no answer.

He dialed 100. It too rang and rang, but no one answered. "Fucking useless bastards!" he screamed. He ran to the kitchen and ran his finger down the list of local numbers stuck to the fridge. He found the number for the local police station and dialed.

"Hello," said a gruff voice.

"Something has happened to my wife. I think she has been attacked!"

"Where, Sir?"

"Next to Palace Grounds. There was a car accident, and they are attacking my wife!"

"Sir, that's not our area. You have to call Shivnagar Police Station. The number is..."

"Fuck you, Fuck you!" John cursed, ending the call.

He grabbed the keys from the kitchen counter-top and ran to the front door. He pulled on his running shoes and unlocked the SUV as he ran toward it. Slamming the vehicle in reverse, he pulled out onto the road, and tires screeching, headed for the main gate. He sounded the horn repeatedly, flashing his lights, and the security guard ran from the guard booth and pulled open the gate as John sped through, barely avoiding running him over. He turned right and sped down the narrow access road, then turned left onto the highway and accelerated as fast as he could. Putting his lights on high beam, he raced south toward the city, thankful there was little traffic at that time of night. Swerving around slower moving lorries and a few late-night taxis, he raced down toward the Hebbal flyover, crossing it at high speed, honking at anyone who came in his way. He flashed his lights continuously, passing cars on the inside when they refused to move across. He sped past Sanjaynagar and down into the underpass at Mekhri Circle, the SUV bottoming out with a sickening thud as it hit the lowest point of the underpass, then climbed up the other side. He would worry about any damage later. He climbed through the gears as he raced up the slope toward Palace Grounds, scanning the road ahead for signs of Charlotte and the car. As the road sloped down the other side, he saw the Toyota on the opposite side of the road, its lights still on, the passenger door open. He slammed his foot on the brake and screeched to a halt. Jumping out of the vehicle, he ran across and vaulted over the central road divider. A body lay curled in the gutter in front of the car, and his heart leaped into his mouth.

"Charlotte!" he screamed and ran toward the body. He crouched down. It wasn't her... it was Sanjay, covered in blood.

"Sanjay, Sanjay! Where is Charlotte?"

Sanjay groaned and opened his eyes. At first, they struggled to focus but then lit up in recognition.

"Sir, I'm so sorry, Sir. Sorry, Sir."

"Where is Charlotte! Where is she?"

"They took her, they took her," and Sanjay lapsed back into unconsciousness.

John sat with his head in his hands. The tears had dried up long ago, replaced first by anger, the anger in turn replaced by frustration, and finally, despair. She was gone, he had no idea where, and he had no idea what to do about it. He was helpless with no one to turn to.

Beside him, in the small private hospital room, Sanjay lay in bed, his head bandaged, tape across his nose, and an IV running into his arm. The tired young doctor, his face displaying the strain of a week of night shifts, had told him Sanjay had a broken nose, several broken ribs, extensive bruising, and a concussion. It would be a while before Sanjay would drive again.

John had picked him up and carried him across the road to his car before driving him to the hospital himself, having little faith an ambulance would arrive in time. He had left Charlotte's Toyota where it had been abandoned by the side of the road, assuming the police would want to take a look at it. But again, he didn't hold out much hope.

With the Hospital's help, he had called the correct Police

Station, and they had promised to send someone around to take a statement. John looked at his watch. It was after two in the morning, yet no one had come yet. In a city of over eight million people with an underpaid overwhelmed Police Force, things didn't move fast.

John rubbed his face and stood, raised his arms above his head, stretching out his back, then walked out into the deserted corridor. He nodded at the lone nurse behind the nurse's station and walked in search of a coffee.

The deserted cafeteria was on the ground floor, just a dozing employee behind the counter. John cleared his throat, and the young boy woke with a start.

"Sir?"

"Coffee, please. Black."

The young boy spooned a portion of instant coffee into a paper cup and filled it with hot water from a large steel urn. John passed over a handful of change and took a sip. Terrible. But at least it was hot, and it might help to keep him going until the police finally arrived. He headed back to the room, and as he walked in, Sanjay stirred and opened his eyes. Seeing John standing beside the bed, he tried to sit up, grimacing as the pain from his broken ribs lanced through his body.

"It's okay, Sanjay. You rest."

"Sir, I'm so sorry, Sir. I couldn't save her, Sir."

John pulled a chair close to the bed and sat down. "Tell me what happened, Sanjay."

Sanjay took a deep breath, wincing with the pain, and composed himself.

"Sir, a car passed us and hit the front of our car. I stopped to see if any damage and to speak to the other driver. There were four of them, Sir. They beat me, kicked me." Sanjay paused, a tear rolling down his cheek. "I was on

the ground, Sir. They kept kicking me, Sir. I couldn't get up."
His voice caught, "And then they took Madam." Tears rolled
down his face, his shoulders shuddering in silent sobs.

John placed his hand over Sanjay's. "It wasn't your fault,
Sanjay." Although if John was honest with himself, he wasn't
sure if he meant what he said. Why did Sanjay have to stop?
If he had kept going, none of this would have happened.
Charlotte would be home, curled up in bed with him.
Maybe it was his own fault? He shouldn't have let Charlotte
go out on her own. He should have been there. He could
have protected her. He should never have taken this posting
in the first place. They should have stayed in England. Grief
welled up inside him, and he shook his head, letting go of
Sanjay's hand. He didn't want to cry in front of Sanjay, so he
stood and paced around the room. He couldn't let himself
think like this. Blame wasn't going to help anyone, and it
certainly wouldn't bring Charlotte back.

He heard a cry at the door and turned to see a small
plump lady in an orange sari, her long hair tied into a
hastily made bun as if she had just got out of bed. She stood
in the doorway her hand over her mouth, tears in her eyes.
Rushing to the bedside, her eyes took in the bandages and
the IV, and she grabbed Sanjay's hand in both of hers and
held it to her chest. She spoke in rapid-fire Kannada, the
local language, as tears streamed from her eyes. Sanjay
looked at John and explained, "My wife, Pournima."

Pournima turned and nodded at John, her lips still
moving in prayer.

Sanjay spoke to her in Kannada, and she paused from
her prayer to reply.

"The doctor called her, Sir. She came as fast as she
could. She had to find someone to look after the children
and a rickshaw to bring her here."

John looked at Pournima, "He will be okay, Pournima."

Pournima looked at John, then back at Sanjay. "She doesn't speak much English, Sir," Sanjay explained. He spoke to Pournima, and the only word John could understand was Madam. Pournima's hand flew to her mouth, and she looked at John in shock, wide-eyed and open-mouthed. She spoke in Kannada, and Sanjay translated.

"She is so sorry about your wife, and she will pray to Amma for her safe return."

John swallowed the grief he was feeling and forced a smile on his face. "Thank you Pournima. Tell her not to worry about the hospital costs. I will pay for everything."

Sanjay turned to look at John, "Thank you so much, Sir, Thank you, thank you." He repeated what John had said to Pournima, and she rushed over to John, taking his hand in hers, her eyes brimming with tears.

"She says she is very grateful."

John and Pournima spent the rest of the night beside Sanjay's bed, dozing off now and then, only to be woken by the night nurse each time she came to check on the patient. It was around five in the morning when two Policemen appeared at the door. One was scruffy, unshaven, with a large belly straining the buttons of his khaki tunic. He appeared to have a mouthful of chewing tobacco—either that or a swollen cheek. The other man, the taller of the two, slim, clean shaven, his uniform clean and well pressed, stepped forward and held out his hand.

"I'm Inspector Rajiv Sampath."

His handshake was firm, and he looked directly into John's eyes. John felt a glimmer of confidence.

"John Hayes." John waved in the direction of the hospital bed. "This is my driver Sanjay and his wife, Pournima."

Inspector Rajiv nodded at them both and turned back to John. "What happened, Mr. Hayes?"

John indicated that Rajiv should sit and sat back down in his chair. Rajiv's scruffy colleague stood in the doorway, his jaw working furiously, the swelling having moved to the other cheek.

John took a deep breath, "Last night my wife and driver were attacked next to Palace Grounds, and she has now disappeared."

Rajiv's eyes narrowed, and he leaned forward, "Can you tell me everything you remember?"

He gestured at the scruffy cop, who came forward and handed him a small, well-used notebook and pen.

"I wasn't there. You will have to ask Sanjay what happened. By the time I got there, it was too late."

"How did you know it was happening?"

"She called me, I was on the phone the whole time..." John's voice broke, tears once again welling in his eyes. "It was terrible!"

"I'm so sorry, Mr. Hayes. My team and I will do everything we can to find Mrs. Hayes. Do you have a photo we can use?"

John removed his wallet from his back pocket and pulled out a small passport sized photo "Only this one from a few years ago. I have more on my phone."

"Okay, I'll give you an email address before I leave. Please email me some recent photos, and we will print them out. In the meantime, I will take a statement from your driver, and we will see what we can do." He turned to Sanjay, questioning him in the local language and scribbling his answers in his notebook while Pournima sat nervously to one side, not letting go of Sanjay's hand. John sat back and watched him work. He seemed professional, certainly more so than the guy with swollen cheeks who still hadn't spoken and was leaning on the door frame, obviously wishing he was somewhere else.

After fifteen to twenty minutes and pages of notes,

Inspector Rajiv stood and handed the notebook and pen to Swollen Cheeks.

"Mr. Hayes, your driver has been helpful. I have an idea of what happened. Unfortunately, he couldn't give much of a description of the people involved, but that's to be expected. It was dark, and he was being beaten. But he did remember part of the car registration and gave me a description of the vehicle. We should be able to narrow it down from that."

John nodded, "How long will it take?"

"We should be able to find out who owns the car within the day. In the meantime, where is your wife's car?"

"It's still there."

"Okay, we will need to impound it as evidence. We will have it towed to our yard at the station. Do you have any other transport?"

"Yes, I have my own car."

"Good. I suggest you go home and grab some rest." He removed a card from the breast pocket of his uniform, passing it to John. "Here's my card. Please call me if you hear anything and don't forget to email me the photos. My email is on the card."

John took out his own card from his wallet and passed it over. "Here's my number, please, please find her for me."

Rajiv took his hand firmly and looked directly into his eyes, "Mr. Hayes, I will do everything in my power to find your wife."

Once the Inspector had left, John returned home to catch a couple of hours sleep. He was physically and emotionally exhausted. There wasn't anything he could do for Sanjay, and he left him with Pournima sitting by his bedside, still holding his hand and praying.

John entered the house and threw the keys into the bowl beside the door. The house felt dark and empty as if missing its soul. John felt the same way. He kicked off his shoes and walked into the living room. Despite the early hour, he poured himself three fingers of gin and drained the glass before refilling it, then flopped down on the sofa, glass in hand. He didn't know what to do, where to look, who to turn to, and he continued blaming himself for not looking after Charlotte. He took another big mouthful of gin, swirling it around in his mouth before swallowing, feeling the warmth spread through his body. Sitting back in the chair, he closed his eyes, the effect of the alcohol and sleepless night taking over and he drifted into a restless sleep.

It was a couple of hours later when he woke with a start,

not sure why he was sleeping on the sofa. His head hurt, and his mouth was dry. The memories came rushing back with a jolt, and he checked his phone for messages. Nothing.

Standing slowly, he stretched, then stumbled listlessly to the kitchen. Running the cold tap in the kitchen sink, he leaned over it and splashed cold water on his face, running his wet fingers through his hair. He needed coffee. He opened the cupboard and removed the French press, measured two heaped spoons of coffee powder into it, and put the kettle on to boil. He stared out into the garden, at the flowers Charlotte had planted, the table and chairs they had set up under the pergola where they used to sit in the early evening when the oppressive heat of the day had eased, sharing a glass of wine or a gin and tonic. In his mind's eye, he could picture her, giggling and tying her long blond hair in a makeshift bun on top of her head, keeping the heat away from her neck. His eyes filled with tears, and he looked away as the kettle clicked off. He filled the French press and left the coffee to brew.

It was almost ten o'clock, and he would normally have been in the office by now. He couldn't face speaking to his colleagues, so he picked up his cell phone and sent a message to David, his boss, telling him he wouldn't be in. He had no desire to speak to anyone and explain what had happened. He just wanted Charlotte back. He couldn't imagine a life without her. He didn't know what to do, so used to having her in the house, her smiles and laughter, the sound of her voice as she sang to herself while painting.

He took Inspector Rajiv's card from his pocket and entered the details into his phone. Scrolling through the pictures on his phone, he selected some recent photos of Charlotte and emailed them to the Inspector. But he had to do more. He had to take control of the situation. He couldn't spend his time sitting around waiting. There had to be something more he could do. He poured himself a coffee and took it upstairs to shower and change.

He ran a hot shower, then turned it to cold, the shock of the cold water waking him up and energizing him—that and the coffee.

A fresh set of clothes on, he went downstairs and grabbed the keys. It was time to visit the Police Station.

9

Shivnagar Police Station was on a busy junction on the boundary of Shivnagar and the neighboring suburb of Shantinagar. A two-story cream-colored, concrete box was the only way to describe it, built for function, not style. In front of the building were rows and rows of two-wheelers, some the property of the policemen and women who worked there, many others confiscated and towed, awaiting their collection by their owners. To the side was a large dirt patch where John parked the SUV. The back of the carpark was filled with rusting shells of cars, held as evidence in traffic accidents, awaiting their time in court. The legal system in India so inundated and backlogged it would be years before many of the cases would be heard. In the meantime, the vehicles rotted away, deteriorating in the alternating extremes of heat and heavy monsoon rain, nature gradually claiming them for her own, creepers and trees growing in and around them. Charlotte's car was already there, dumped to one side, the sight of it bringing a lump to his throat.

John stepped out of his car and walked across the

carpark and into the entrance hall of the station. It was a square room as wide as it was long, filled with people, most sitting on the rows of tired wooden seats running along each side wall. At the end of the room, facing the entrance, stood a wide desk, piled high with files. Battered filing cabinets lined the walls behind, their tops piled high in yet more files and papers bound together with rubber bands and weighed down with paperweights. A ceiling fan rotated at high speed, providing scant respite from the heat outside.

A uniformed constable sat behind the desk, attending to the queue of people lined up before him. He spotted John, the lone westerner, at the end of the queue and waved him forward.

"Sir, can I help you?"

"My name is John Hayes, I've come to see Inspector Rajiv Sampath."

"One moment, Sir." He turned in his chair and shouted a name over his shoulder.

Another policeman popped his head around the corner.

"Tell Rajiv Sir, Mr. Hayes is here to see him."

The policeman disappeared, and the desk officer turned back to John, "Please wait, Sir." He waved to the seating at the side and went back to dealing with the people in the queue. Five minutes passed, and the policeman came out, and John followed him through a side door and down a corridor to a closed door. The policeman tapped on the door, and a voice called out, "Enter."

John walked in behind the constable into a large room. In contrast to the reception area, the room was air-conditioned and cool, the walls covered in framed photos of a senior police officer shaking hands with VIPs and cutting ribbons.

At the end of the room, with its back to the window, was

a large polished wooden desk, its surface devoid of anything but a small Indian flag, a few sheets of paper, and a mobile phone. Behind the desk sat a police officer in starched khaki. He was, what would locally be described as 'healthily' built, his face on the verge of puffy, and despite obviously being in the latter part of middle-age, his hair was so black, the color could only have come from a bottle. He stood with considerable effort, and after taking a breath, smiled at John, his belly straining to escape the confines of his uniform shirt.

"Mr. Hayes," he leaned over the desk and extended his hand. "Please, take a seat." He waved to one of two chairs in front of the desk.

"Shivraj," he called to the constable, "Bring us some tea."

John sat down and waited for the senior police officer to be seated.

"I am Senior Police Inspector Basavraj Muniappa." He introduced himself as if proud of his name and rank. "I am in charge of this station and will be overseeing your case. I am very sorry to hear what has happened, and I can assure you we are doing everything we can to find her."

There was a tap on the door behind John. Inspector Rajiv entered, nodded at John, then stood beside the desk.

S.P.I Muniappa flicked his eyes in Rajiv's direction. "Inspector Sampath is my best man, and he is doing everything he can to find her."

Inspector Rajiv spoke up, "Mr. Hayes, I am making copies of the photos you sent me and distributing them to all the other police stations in Bangalore. We have also briefed our patrolling constables, and they are going door to door in the surrounding area, making inquiries."

John nodded and asked, "What about the car? Have you traced it yet?"

Rajiv hesitated, about to reply, but before he could speak, the senior inspector cut him off with a glance, "We are still making inquiries, Mr. Hayes, and as soon as we find it, we will let you know."

Rajiv closed his mouth and frowned.

"There must be something I can do? It's been twelve hours since it happened, and you still have no leads. I'm just supposed to sit around and wait?"

"Mr. Hayes, I'm sorry, but there is really nothing you can do. You don't speak the language, and we have our best men on the job. Please go home, rest, and we will be in touch as soon as anything develops."

He stood, his smile not extending to his eyes, and held out his hand again. John rose, shook his hand, and glanced across at Rajiv. Rajiv's eyes flicked toward Muniappa and returned to John with an almost imperceptible shake of his head.

10

I t was the sitting around waiting that was frustrating him. Not knowing where she was, whether or not she was okay, made him feel helpless, less of a man. Not only had he failed to protect her, but he had no idea how to get her back. He should have stayed at home in safe old England where he knew the language, where things functioned the way he was used to. Here, he didn't even know where to start. He cursed the day he chose to take up this job.

His meeting earlier in the day with Senior Inspector Muniappa troubled him. There was something not quite right. John couldn't put his finger on it, but he didn't trust the man, sure he was hiding something, not telling him the complete truth.

Inspector Rajiv though was a different kettle of fish. He exuded a quiet confidence, seemed like a man who could get things done. There was something going on during the meeting, an undercurrent, and John made a mental note to ask him about it the next time he met him alone. In the meantime, all he could do was wait.

He poured himself another generous measure of gin from the sideboard, knocking back a large mouthful before resuming his seat in the armchair staring at the wall. The neat spirit, his fourth since he had returned from the police station, warmed the back of his throat but did nothing to dull the pain in his chest.

The shadows lengthened in the garden outside as the sun prepared to retire for the night, the day passing without him noticing. John checked his phone again, ignoring the messages from work, but there was nothing from Rajiv. The only call had been one from the security guard at the front gate, requesting permission to send a television news crew in, a request he had denied. He had no idea how they had tracked him down. If only the police were as efficient.

He put the phone to charge and took another swig of his drink. Food would be good, but the truth was he had no appetite and lacked any motivation to make anything, anyway. Instead, he reached for the television remote and flicked on the TV, scrolling through the channels until he stopped on a news station. It was the usual rubbish, one political party blaming another for myriad evils, the latest gossip from Bollywood, a cricketer rumored to be dating a local starlet. He didn't pay much attention at first, letting the noise waft over him, the light from the TV flickering through the darkening room. It was only when a picture of a silver Audi appeared in the corner of the screen behind the presenter that John leaned forward, increasing the volume with the remote.

"Police are investigating the disappearance of Mrs. Charlotte Hayes in Bangalore after an altercation last night near the posh suburb of Shivnagar. Mrs. Hayes was returning home with her driver late yesterday evening when her car met with an accident. We understand four men in a silver

Audi A6 assaulted her and her driver before kidnapping Mrs. Hayes. Her current whereabouts are unknown. Police are investigating. Swati Chandrashekar reporting from Shivnagar."

The camera switched to a young lady standing in front of a pair of iron gates while a group of men jostled behind her, each desperate to get into the camera frame. In her left hand, she held a large microphone while her right hand was pressed to her ear.

"Thank you, Rahul. Last night Mrs. Hayes, an expatriate English woman was violently assaulted not far from here. Her driver is currently recovering in hospital after being viciously beaten. Doctors say his condition is stable, but he will need to remain in the hospital for some time. Mrs. Hayes' current whereabouts are unknown, and it is feared she has been kidnapped by her assailants. We tried reaching out to Mrs. Hayes' husband, John Hayes, an English expat who works for an overseas bank but have been unable to contact him. An unnamed source at Shivnagar Police station claims the Audi A6 driven by the assailants is registered to Surya Patil, leader of the Progressive People's Alliance and a Member of the Legislative Assembly, whose residence lies behind me. Mr. Patil could not be reached for comment. However, a spokesperson for Mr. Patil claims the car was reported stolen early yesterday evening and has not been found. Police are continuing to make inquiries."

The camera switched back to the studio. "Thank you, Swati, and in other news..."

John switched off the TV and sat back in the chair, staring at the blank screen. So, they do know who the car belongs to. He reached for his phone and scrolled through for Rajiv's number and dialed.

It rang twice.

"Hello."

"Inspector Sampath, this is John Hayes."

"Yes, Mr. Hayes, I'm sorry I still don't have any news for you."

"But I just saw the news. They said the car was registered to a Surya Patil."

Inspector Rajiv didn't answer immediately.

"Hello?" John thought he had got cut off. He heard a sigh.

"Yes, Mr. Hayes, it's not supposed to be public knowledge. This type of media speculation does not help us with our inquiries."

"But does it belong to him? Is he involved?"

"Mr. Hayes, our inquiries are ongoing. Mr. Patil says the car was stolen and there is certainly no sign of the vehicle at his residence. I think it highly unlikely he would be involved, anyway. He is an older man, very prominent in State politics. He has a driver, a man like him never drives himself, and he would have too much to lose doing something like this. We are still investigating, and I will let you know as soon as we make any progress."

"Okay, please do, thank you." John hung up and put the phone down on the table. Inspector Rajiv sounded confident, but John's gut told him something wasn't right

Had the car actually been stolen or was it all a coverup? John had spent enough time in India to know what one saw on the news was not always the absolute truth. Maybe the Minister was involved, despite the denials? It was the only lead John had. He made a decision. Walking to the kitchen, he ran the kitchen tap and splashed cold water on his face before pouring himself a glass of water. He felt fresher as if he now had a purpose. Whether it was right or wrong, he couldn't sit around and do nothing, he needed to take action. Retrieving his car keys from the bowl by the front door, he marched out.

11

S urya Patil sat behind the large polished wooden desk in his study and glared at the young man standing in front of him, making no attempt to hide his contempt.

The young man shifted uneasily, moving his weight from one foot to the other, his eyes fixed firmly on the desk, unwilling to make eye contact.

Surya was a tough man. He had come up the hard way, and it influenced everything he did. In his mind, life was black and white... there are predators, and there is prey. Everything he did, every decision he made were all designed to make sure he remained a predator and held on to his position at the top of the food chain. Born to a poor farmer in a North Karnataka village, he grew up an only child, his sole sibling having died in infancy. His father scratched out a meager living on a small plot of land, growing millets and pulses, but frequent droughts meant harvests failed regularly, and there had been many times when they had nothing to eat. Eventually, Surya's father, unable to cope with crippling debt and an overwhelming sense of failure, drank a liter of weed killer, painfully ending his life on the very land that had failed to support them.

From that day forward, Surya vowed never to be poor again. Leaving his mother alone with her grief, he had caught a ride on a lorry headed south for Bangalore, finding whatever work he could—mopping floors in restaurants and chopping onions and peeling potatoes. He had progressed to waiting tables, learning English from customers, and saving his tips. Eventually, he saved enough to buy a second-hand car which he operated as a taxi, over time expanding to more vehicles and eventually, buses. His company, one of the largest transport companies in the State, now had contracts with most of the software companies in Bangalore, transporting thousands of IT professionals around the city. It was an incredible achievement for anyone, let alone a poor man from the village, but it hadn't been enough for him. He craved more wealth and power, and in India, the quickest way to get that is to enter politics. Surya joined the Progressive People's Alliance Party, using generous donations to gain a foothold in the party ranks, combining his street smarts and a killer instinct to ruthlessly crush anyone who stood in his path to the top. He had been the Party Leader for over ten years now, and his wealth and influence had grown exponentially. He no longer needed the income from his transport business, but the manpower the company provided meant one call from him and he could halt all transport to the major employers of the city, dealing a crippling blow to his foes. That amount of leverage and influence was something he would never give up. One final goal remained though—Chief Minister of his State. Then no one could send him back to the fields, and his family, for generations to come, would never be poor again. That would be his legacy. The young man standing before him, however, could put all his plans in danger.

"Do you have anything to say?"

The young man shrugged.

"My phone is ringing off the hook. The police are calling about my car, a woman has gone missing. TV reporters are calling asking for comments, our house is on the news, and you have nothing to say?"

Sunil Patil, the only son of the great businessman and politician Surya Patil, just shook his head.

Surya breathed out in exasperation. He had spent a fortune on his son, sent him to the best schools, bought him everything he wanted, indulged his every whim, made sure he wanted for nothing. No child of his should have a childhood as brutal as his own. But what did he have to show for his generosity? A twenty-five-year-old son, who didn't get out of bed until noon, spent his days idling around the house, and his evenings drinking in bars with a group of equally idle and entitled friends. He frowned and leaned forward on the desk.

"So, how did the car get stolen?"

No reply.

"Answer me!" Surya roared.

Sunil flinched. Despite his age, he was still scared of his father. Surya Patil was an imposing man at the best of times and terrifying when he was angry.

"I don't know, Father," Sunil mumbled.

"Speak up!"

Sunil cleared his throat, "I parked it on Church Street, and when I came back, it was gone."

"What were you doing in Church Street? Drinking again?"

Sunil nodded.

"Where?"

"A couple of places."

"And you planned to drive home?"

Sunil nodded almost imperceptibly, knowing what was to follow.

Surya slammed his fist down on the desk, the shockwave sending a pen rolling across the surface and onto the floor.

"Are you a complete idiot? I have fought tooth and nail to get where I am today. I have built a lot of power and influence in this town to provide for you and the family. Do you even have any idea of what it was like for me growing up? To have no food? To hear my mother crying every night? Do you?"

Sunil shook his head although he had heard this argument many times before. "No, Father."

"And you have nothing to do with this woman who has disappeared?"

Sunil shook his head.

"I've given you everything you ever wanted, you have a life I could only dream of at your age, and this is how you repay me?"

Sunil tried to make himself as small as possible, unable to look his father in the eye.

"How many times have I had to bail you out in the past because of your stupidity? You are an idiot! A spoiled good-for-nothing idiot! I am ashamed to call you my son. Now I have to clean up yet another mess of yours. Get out of my sight!"

Sunil turned and scurried out of the room as Surya sat back in his chair. He could feel a headache coming on, and he rubbed his temples with his fingers. Swiveling his chair, he turned around and looked out the window. Lights were starting to come on across the suburb as dusk fell on the homes of the city's rich and powerful. Surya had fought hard in his climb to the top, stepped on a lot of toes, made a lot of enemies—all for his family. Not for the first time, he wondered if it was all worth it.

There was no love in his marriage, his wife spent most of her time and his money in Dubai, buying endless amounts of handbags and had so much plastic surgery, she was unrecognizable from the young village girl he had fallen in love with so many years ago.

And his useless son? He had wanted so much for him to follow in his footsteps, but Sunil would never be half the man he was. If it hadn't been for Surya's influence and connections, Sunil would have been in prison a long time ago, serving time for myriad assaults, drug possession, and drunk and disorderly behavior. He hoped to God Sunil had nothing to do with the foreign woman's disappearance.

Surya sighed and turned back to his desk to make the necessary calls. It was sad to admit to himself, but even though he was one of the most powerful and successful men in Bangalore, his personal life was a failure.

12

The evening rush hour had started, the traffic a maddening mass of honking chaos, and it took John a good forty minutes to travel the ten kilometers to Shivnagar. He used the time to think. He didn't know the actual address of the Minister, but the image of the house and its gate was imprinted in his brain. Shivnagar wasn't a big suburb, and it was laid out in a grid-like pattern so he would drive every street if he had to. He entered from the northwest corner, slowing as he did so and scanned each side of the street, ignoring the honking from behind him. The drivers behind him eventually giving up and overtaking, gesticulating angrily as they passed. Ignoring them, John reached the end and turned left, heading west to east, all the while looking at the houses on each side of the street. Many wealthy businessmen and politicians made the suburb their home, and the houses here were huge—three, four and five stories, many built to the extreme edge of their plots, using every piece of ground available. The politicians' houses were easily identifiable with their security guards outside, and often, even at this late hour, with lines of people waiting outside the gates for an audience. The cars in the street were fancier too—Mercedes, BMWs, Audis. John shook his head. So much for honest politicians. None of this was affordable on a government salary, but they didn't even try to hide it. He turned left again, heading north to complete three-quarters of his circumnavigation, but there was still no sign of the house he wanted although many looked similar.

He turned left again, driving east to west, completing the circuit, then started to work his way inwards, crisscrossing the suburb, driving every street, ensuring he didn't miss anything. He had been driving for fifteen minutes, starting to despair when he saw it. It was just as he had seen on the television but minus the news crew. The big iron gates were slightly ajar, a heavy-set man standing beside the gate, another elderly man sitting on a plastic chair on the footpath. Both wore the uniforms of security guards—black pants and grey shirts with epaulets. The older man even had a beret pulled down tightly over his head. John slowed and looked through the gap in the gate. The house was set back from the road, and a white S Class Mercedes with tinted windows and a large white Toyota Land Cruiser were parked in front of it. The house towered four stories above the garden, whitewashed with a full-width balcony on each floor. Red flowering bougainvillea cascaded from the planter boxes lining the balconies, providing a splash of vibrant color against the plain white walls. John reached the end of the street and made a U-turn before driving back. Now he had found the house, he didn't know what to do next, having acted purely on impulse. There was no sign of the Audi, but what did he expect? It had been reported stolen. There was no connection otherwise with the owner. But John couldn't sit around doing nothing. Charlotte was still out there somewhere, and he had to find her. He needed to do something, or at the very least, feel like he was doing something.

John pulled up near the house and parked on the opposite side of the road, switching off the ignition. The security guards glanced in his direction but paid him no attention, going back to their conversation, the standing guard pausing to spit a long stream of red colored spittle at the foot of a nearby tree.

John picked up his phone from the seat beside him and looked at the screen saver. Charlotte smiled back at him in a photo taken when they were in Goa eight months before. Her skin was tanned golden, and her already blonde hair lightened further by the sun. Tears welled in his eyes, and he swallowed as a lump formed in his throat. He had to be strong. He put the phone in his back pocket and climbed out of his SUV, closing the door behind him. Automatically, he pressed the button on the key fob, locking the car with an electronic blip, the sound alerting the security guards, both looking up curiously, then going back to their conversation. John took a deep breath, then crossed the road and walked toward them.

As John approached, the seated guard, a thin man in his sixties, looked up and nudged the other guard. The standing guard was younger, perhaps in his thirties with a big belly. He turned to face John, and as he approached, he spat another long stream of red spittle at the base of the tree. Judging by the color of the tree trunk, it was a regular habit.

John nodded at them both and attempted to walk past and through the gates. The fat guard moved to block his way.

"*Yen beku*? What do you want?"

"I want to speak to the owner, Mr. Patil," John replied.

Fat Guard glanced at the seated guard, then looked back at John, switching to English. "Sir is not available."

"Is he home?" John asked.

"He is not available," came the reply.

John looked at the seated guard who was studying him with a frown on his face, then looked back at Fat Guard. He took another deep breath, composed himself.

"I want to speak to your boss. It's very important. I am going inside." He stepped to one side and made as if to walk through the gate.

Fat Guard placed his hand on John's chest and pushed him back away from the gate. The older guard stood up and pulled out a battered Nokia phone from his pocket and started dialing.

"Sir is not available," Fat Guard repeated, pushing John back toward the curb.

"Get your hands off me!" John grabbed his wrist and pulled it away from his chest. Fat Guard moved closer, his face just inches away from John. He turned his head slightly and spat the contents of his mouth onto the pavement, red liquid and spittle splashing onto John's shoes. He turned back to John, his teeth and gums stained red, the smell of his foul breath mixing with the sour smell of stale sweat from his unwashed uniform.

"Go!"

He stepped forward, so close now, his large belly pressed up against John. John pushed him back, anger welling up inside him as the adrenaline pumped through his veins. He hated bullies, and this guy was one, used to pushing people around. John shoved him backward.

"I'm going inside." He moved toward the gate, just as two

young men stepped out from inside and blocked the
entrance. John looked them over. They were big, had obviously spent time in the gym in the past but had since gone
soft with layers of fat covering the muscle they had built.
They both sneered at John, arrogance oozing from their
pores.

By now John was too angry to think sensibly. His hands
were trembling with the energy coursing through his veins,
a red mist before his eyes, the reason for being there forgotten. He was not going to be pushed around. He stepped
again closer to the gate but felt someone grabbing his left
arm. He turned to pull it free and felt a blow to his stomach.
It took all the air out of him, and he doubled up in pain,
dropping to one knee, trying to catch his breath as tears
welled up in his eyes. He looked up and saw the men grinning at him.

"Bastards," he gasped and pushed himself up to a
standing position. "You think you are men because four of
you can push me around!" One of them, perhaps Fat Guard,
shoved him from behind, and he stumbled forward into the
two younger men. They pushed him back, still grinning.
Hands grabbed his arms from behind, then one of the men
stepped forward, pushing his face into John's.

"Fuck off," he snarled, and then punched John again in
the gut. John collapsed to the ground, gasping for breath. He
heard a snigger, he didn't know who it was, he couldn't look
up this time, the pain was too much, and he was having
trouble breathing.

A vehicle honked, and he sensed movement around
him. He looked up and saw the men, including the two
guards, moving behind the gate, pulling it shut. John rose
from his knees to his feet, finally able to catch his breath as a

white Mahindra Bolero SUV with police markings pulled up at the curb.

The passenger door opened, and Inspector Rajiv stepped out. "Mr. Hayes, are you ok? Quick, get in the car." He opened the rear passenger door and guided John inside before getting in beside him. Rajiv nodded at the policeman in the driver's seat who pulled away from the curb and turned right at the end of the street. Rajiv sat back and studied John in silence, John not saying anything, just looking down at his hands, still trembling as the adrenaline sought an outlet. Rajiv turned to the driver, told him something in the local language, and the driver pulled to the curb, switched the engine off and got out. John and Rajiv watched him as he crossed the street and leaned against a tree, pulling a packet of cigarettes from his back pocket and lighting one.

John sensed he was about to be told something and preferred not to be the first to speak.

"Mr. Hayes, what were you doing?" Rajiv finally asked.

"How did you know?" John countered.

"I heard it on the radio. Someone from the house phoned the station."

John remembered the old guard with the Nokia. He nodded.

"What were you doing, Mr. Hayes?"

"I saw the news reports saying the car was registered to Surya Patil. I came to speak to him."

"Mr. Patil reported the car stolen."

John looked heavily at Rajiv. "Is that really true? Or is it a cover-up?"

Rajiv hesitated and looked out the window for a moment. He continued, his eyes on the driver, "Mr. Hayes, here in India, politicians are very powerful people. They are untouchable by the law, and by extension, those who work for them consider themselves untouchable by the law as well." He turned back to face John.

"You saw how you were treated just now. Do you think there is anything I can do to prevent them hitting you? I can arrest them, and they will be out within an hour. And what is worse is I may get suspended for taking action against them. I can't help find Mrs. Hayes if I am suspended."

"You are not answering my question."

Rajiv sighed. "We have to assume the car was stolen until we find any evidence to the contrary. We have nothing linking Mr. Patil or anyone who works for him to this case. The car is missing. It was reported stolen yesterday. That's all we know." Rajiv paused and looked at John.

"I like you, Mr. Hayes. I want to help you. I am doing everything I can to find your wife. But you have to realize, things happen differently here. There are ways of doing things, and justice is not always clear-cut. If Mr. Patil or anyone who works for him is involved, I will find out.

"But be warned, these are powerful people. If you upset them, you could meet with an unfortunate accident." He paused, "They can make you disappear, and no one will ever find out why or where." He reached over and put his hand on John's arm.

"Be careful, Mr. Hayes. Please now go home and get some rest. I will have my driver drop you off. Give me your keys, and I'll have your car delivered to your house in a couple of hours."

"I can't just sit by and do nothing while I know Charlotte is out there. I need to help her."

"Mr. Hayes... there is nothing you can do. I am doing

everything I can. I have my men out making inquiries. We will find her. Now, give me your keys."

Rajiv wound down the window and called out to his driver before turning back to John. "Oh, and Mr. Hayes, next time you have a few drinks, please at least attempt to disguise the smell on your breath before driving."

13

Sunil Patil stood beside the fourth-floor window, watching the scene at the gate unfold. He had been alerted by the shouting and curious, walked to the window of his top floor living room. From there, he had a clear view of the front gate, and he watched as a foreign man attempted to enter. The guards were under strict instructions to never let anyone in unless they had a prior appointment, and they enjoyed enforcing the rule. In India, it seemed everyone was the boss of someone else. It was a complicated hierarchy, but there was always someone you could push around, no matter what your station in life. The guards felt they had the same power as his father and had no compunction in throwing their weight about. Sunil usually found it amusing to watch, but this time he was worried. He picked up the cigarette packet from the window sill and tapped one out, lighting it from a gold Zippo. He took a drag and blew a long cloud of smoke into the air.

The shouts in the street were getting louder, and now, his father's driver and bodyguard had become involved. It was unusual because Westerners rarely came to see his father at the house, preferring instead to keep up appearances of professionalism by meeting in hotels where they exchanged briefcases full of money in return for permits and permissions.

It could just be a coincidence, but the fact this Westerner was here the day after his fun with the little English whore gave him cause for concern. If the man was her husband, he had made the connection with Sunil way too quickly. Those fucking journalists and their big mouths! Sunil had seen the reports on the TV regarding his car, but he was confident no one would ever find it. By now, the Audi was being stripped down across the border in Tamil Nadu, the parts being shipped and sold all over the country and could never be traced back to him. It was a pity, he had liked the car, but with the amount of money that flowed through his family's hands, it was easily replaced. Besides, most of the car dealers owed his father a favor.

The foreigner was now on his knees gasping for breath, having taken a number of hard blows to the stomach. That would teach him to come around to his house. Sunil's satisfied smirk soon disappeared as he saw the police Bolero enter the street and pull up outside the gate, the guards wisely coming back inside and leaving the foreigner on the footpath. The cops could never do anything to the men who worked for his father, but there was no point in provoking them unnecessarily.

A tall, slim police officer got out of the vehicle and bent down to help the foreigner to his feet. Sunil couldn't hear what was being said, but he made a mental note of the cop's face. He had seen him around before in the area and often at political gatherings looking after the police security. He had never had to deal with him though, their paths never crossing which pointed to the cop as one of the honest ones. Sunil knew all the dishonest cops, always with their hands out. No, this guy he would have to be careful of, he thought as he watched the white police vehicle pull away from the house.

14

On the northern edge of Bangalore lies the five-hundred-acre campus of the Gandhi Krishi Vignana Kendra or GKVK as it's known locally. A beautiful tree-filled expanse of green which not only serves as the main agricultural university in Karnataka but also as a much-needed green lung amongst the urban sprawl. Once alone and surrounded by countryside, it had now been enveloped as the city spread its concrete tentacles north toward the international airport.

At six o'clock in the morning, the campus was surprisingly busy, not so much with students although late night revelers staggering back to the hostels were not an uncommon sight. Instead, the majority of the early morning crowd is made up of the general public—morning walkers, dog owners, and runners—making use of the network of trails. It provided a beautiful and much-needed escape from the congestion and hustle and bustle of the city.

Satyanarayan Rao loved to start his day there as he had for the last eight years, a routine which began when the family took delivery of a Labrador pup they had named Jackson after his two daughters' favorite pop-star, Michael. The girls doted on their dog, but inevitably, the task of daily exercise fell on Mr. Rao, the girls preferring to stay in bed at that time of the morning. Jackson was getting on in age now and a few kilos overweight, but he still wagged his tail and jumped up and down with excitement as soon as he saw Mr. Rao putting on his dusty old trainers. The house was just one street away from GKVK, and it was only a five-minute walk before they squeezed through a gap in the stone boundary wall and were on the grounds themselves. Mr. Rao and Jackson had a regular route, one they followed every day. Mr. Rao was not the type of man who liked to change his routine. From the gap in the wall, they took a well-trod dirt path down to one of the main internal roads which they followed for a kilometer before turning off and taking another hard-beaten dirt track which wound its way through fields of sunflowers, then around the back of the student hostels and into the mango orchards. The trees were full of birds flitting back and forth—mynahs, bulbuls, ring-necked doves, and occasionally, a peacock. Some walkers had mentioned spotting wild pigs and even a deer, but Mr. Rao had never come across anything that big, in fact, nothing larger than a mongoose or a hare. He always carried a stick though, just in case he came across a snake or a pack of stray dogs. He had been lucky so far, the presence of Jackson ensuring most wildlife scattered long before he came along.

As the sun rose above the horizon and the temperature increased, Mr. Rao paused to remove the light outer jacket he was wearing, tying it around his waist, then resumed his walk, taking a left fork in the path leading away from the mango orchards into the sapota orchard. Sapotas or

Chikkus as they were more commonly known were not a favorite of Mr. Rao, but his daughters loved them and always begged him to bring some back during the season. He occasionally did, and he looked around now for some ripe ones. Just one or two, whatever he could hide in his pocket. Although there wasn't much security on duty this early in the morning, he didn't want to be banned from visiting GKVK for stealing fruit.

Jackson was no longer in sight, but he wasn't worried. The dog often ran off to explore but always rejoined Mr. Rao at some stage of the walk. He continued on, humming to himself, enjoying the fresh air and the sounds of nature. This time alone, before he had to get the girls ready for school and head to the office, gave him so much pleasure, the morning walk always setting him up to have a good day.

The path wound its way between the trees and up a gentle slope and after cresting a low brow led down to a pond, completely dry at this time of the year, just a depression in the ground filled with long-dried mud, riven with cracks and gullies. Jackson barked, and he saw him ahead, on the path at the other side of the pond, looking back at him and wagging his tail. The dog turned toward the undergrowth beside the path and barked again before looking back at Mr. Rao.

"What is it, boy? What have you found?"

Jackson barked again, and this time, whined but refused to move away from the spot.

"Come here, boy,"

Mr. Rao approached the bushes cautiously, wary of the snake or whatever it was that had seized Jackson's attention. Jackson was staring into the undergrowth, whining with excitement, and Mr. Rao bent down and patted Jackson on the head.

"What is it, boy?" He turned and looked in the direction of Jackson's gaze. There was something of color in the bushes. Using his stick, he parted the branches and peered inside.

"*Hey Bhagwan*!" he cried and dropped his stick in shock.

15

It was just after nine a.m. when they knocked on his door. John had slept late after a night drinking in front of the television.

He woke with a dull throbbing in his temples, his mouth and throat dry. It took a while for him to orient himself, not sure what had woken him or why he was on the couch, but then it all came flooding back—the grief, the despair, the helplessness.

A banging on the door roused him from the depths of self-pity, and he swung his legs onto the floor and pulled himself off the sofa, still dressed in the previous day's clothes.

At the front door, two grim-faced uniformed constables stood on the bottom step looking up at him.

"Can I help you?"

"Mr. John Hayes?"

"Yes, what is it?" John had a bad feeling.

"Mr. Hayes, we need you to come with us. We have found a body matching your wife's description, and we would like you to please come and take a look." John's legs gave way, and he collapsed to the floor.

Thirty minutes later, he was sitting in the back seat of the police jeep, heading south from his home into Bangalore City. The constables had been kind. They picked him up off the floor and sat him down while one of them made a pot of strong coffee. John had asked for more details, but they told him they didn't know anymore, and Inspector Rajiv would meet him at the hospital.

It was the same hospital where he had taken the driver, all too familiar now. The jeep pulled into the forecourt and double-parked, and as John got out of the vehicle, a somber-looking Inspector Rajiv walked out.

"Mr. Hayes, thank you for coming. I wish it was under better circumstances."

"Is it her?" John was scared to hear the answer.

Rajiv took a deep breath. "It's better you come and see."

John followed him inside, through the waiting room, and down a long corridor leading toward the rear of the hospital. Rajiv paused beside a closed door, looked back at John, then opened the door.

The room was cold and empty. Harsh fluorescent lights shone down from the ceiling on the sole piece of furniture, a hospital bed in the center of the room. On it was a long shape covered by a white sheet. Rajiv walked to one end of the bed and turned to John.

"Mr. Hayes, are you ready?"

John swallowed and nodded from his position by the door, too scared to approach closer.

Rajiv pulled the sheet back and looked back with concern toward John.

For the second time that morning, John collapsed on the floor.

16

John stood at the entrance to the living room and looked around. Along one wall, stacked cardboard boxes were filled with the remains of a life once shared, and in the middle of the room more boxes waiting to be filled. The walls were now bare, and the sofa and one of the armchairs were pushed to one end of the room. The room was almost finished, just the television and the other armchair remained in their usual place. John had been back for two weeks, but his time in the city was nearing its end. There were too many bad memories, and he had no desire to stay on. The company had given him time off on compassionate grounds, and he had accompanied Charlotte's body back to Winchester to give her the burial she deserved. The church had been filled to capacity, she had been well-loved and was sorely missed by all who knew her. Hundreds of friends and well-wishers filed past her coffin, paying their respects, the makeup and clothing doing a great job of hiding her bruises and injuries, giving no visible indication of her violent end. The wake afterward had been painful, and John didn't bother to hang around, slipping out the back door of his in-law's house and returning to his hotel room where he had descended into an alcohol-filled abyss of self-pity that had taken weeks to climb out of. Even now, he was drinking too much and had not slept a full night in months.

Despite a media frenzy in the week following the discovery of her body, it had all eventually died down, and her attackers had never been caught. The news-hungry public moved on to equally despicable acts in other locations. The police had told him they were still investigating, but their reports were few and far between, and the last time he had seen Rajiv, he had been reluctant to meet John's eyes.

There was one room in the house he hadn't even begun to pack up yet. John hadn't been able to face it, putting it off until the last minute, but he couldn't postpone it any longer. Gritting his teeth, John climbed the stairs and walked down the hall to what had been Charlotte's studio, a room he hadn't entered since she was murdered. Steeling himself, he pushed down on the door handle and stepped inside.

The almost completed landscape sat on the easel in the center of the room, exactly as it had the last time they had been in here together. The sight of the canvases and the smell of her watercolors triggered so many memories, her life force seemingly still present in the room despite six months passing. Bitterness filled John's throat, replacing the constant feeling of despair. He should never have brought her to this city. It was all his fault.

They had both wanted adventure and were excited about being posted in India, but John was the one who had really pushed it. He clenched his fists, the rage building in his body, seeking an outlet. He grabbed her stool from in front of the easel and with an anguished roar, hurled it across the room where it bounced off the wall, one of its legs snapping in half. He grabbed the edge of the table and flipped it over, scattering paints and brushes across the floor. John stomped on the brushes where they lay, snapping them underfoot, then moved to pick up the easel, ready to smash it into a thousand pieces. He grabbed the frame and raised it above his head, then stopped, realizing what he was doing, his rage spent. He placed it back on the ground and dropped to his knees, overcome with grief, sobbing.

"I'm so sorry, I'm so sorry..."

It was a while later when he woke, curled in a fetal position on the floor. His left arm had gone numb, and the side of his face was cold where it had been pressed against the marble floor. He felt empty as if all emotion had been drained from his soul. Rubbing his eyes and face, he sat up and looked around the room at the broken chair, the table on its side, and the detritus of scattered paints and broken brushes. John stood and picked up the chair with its broken leg and placed it in the corner. He righted the table and sighed. He was never coming back. Once the house was packed up, he was going home. He had already resigned from his job, unable to continue in the same office or indeed working with the same people, news of Charlotte's death having spread company-wide. Even during his visit to the London office before returning to Bangalore, he had felt the pitying glances of his colleagues as he walked through the building. He needed a fresh start, away from all these memories. He would pack up Charlotte's paintings and send them to her parents. All the paintings, bar one—the unfinished one that now sat on the easel, a reminder of their last holiday together in Ooty.

That evening, he was sitting in the darkened living room, a drink in his hand, when he heard a knock on the door. He ignored it at first, he wasn't expecting anyone, but the knocking persisted. Reluctantly, he got to his feet and went to open it.

On the front step stood Sanjay, a cloth carry bag in his hand, his face breaking into a smile when he saw John.

"Sir, how are you?"

John arranged his face into a reluctant half smile, replacing his look of surprise. "I'm okay, Sanjay, come on in."

Sanjay slipped off his sandals and walked in, his eyes darting around the house, noticing the piled boxes.

"Sir, you are leaving?"

John turned on the lights in the living room and gestured for Sanjay to sit down. He pushed the other armchair toward the center of the room, but Sanjay shook his head and remained standing. John stood too, resting his hands on the back of the armchair, feeling uncomfortable about sitting while Sanjay remained on his feet.

"Yes, Sanjay. I can't stay. I'm going back to England. How are you? Fully recovered?"

"Yes, Sir. Thank you, Sir. And thank you for paying for the hospital, Sir."

"Don't mention it Sanjay. It's the least I can do. You looked after Madam and me very well."

At the mention of Charlotte, tears welled up in Sanjay's eyes, and he looked down at his feet and swallowed. John watched him, saying nothing, giving him time. Gaining control over his emotions, Sanjay looked up again.

"What will you do now, Sir?"

"I don't know, Sanjay. I will go back to England, take some time off, maybe travel a bit."

"Yes, Sir, keep yourself busy." He nodded enthusiastically. "My missus made this for you." Sanjay reached into the carry bag and removed a stainless-steel food container handing it over to John.

"It's mutton curry and *dosas*. She thought you might be hungry."

"That's so kind of her, Sanjay, please thank her for me. Can I get you some tea?"

Sanjay shook his head and looked down at his feet again. "Ah, Sir..."

"What is it Sanjay?"

Sanjay reached into his pants pocket and pulled out a folded piece of newspaper. He unfolded it carefully and held it out.

"What is it?"

"Sir, please take a look."

John placed the food container on the armchair and took the paper from Sanjay. It was taken from the society pages of the Deccan Herald, a black-and-white photograph of a young man smiling at the camera, accompanied by three other men and two young women. It appeared to have been taken at a restaurant opening.

John looked up, "What's this, Sanjay?"

"He was there, Sir." He pointed at the young man. "Him, Sir. That night when Madam..."

John looked at the photo again and read the caption beneath it. *Sunil Patil and friends celebrate the opening of Bombay Talkies, a new restaurant in Indiranagar.*

"Are you sure Sanjay?"

"Yes, I'm sure, Sir. And those men beside him. I think they were there too."

"We have to tell the police, Sanjay. With you as a witness, they can arrest these men."

Sanjay shook his head violently, "No, Sir, please. These people... you don't know what they can do. Sunil Patil's father is Surya Patil, the Minister. He is rich and extremely powerful."

"But Sanjay, they have broken the law. The police can arrest them."

"Sir, things don't work like that here. The politicians control the police, and if they found out I know who it was, they will have me killed. Who will look after my children?" he clasped his hands in front of him, "No, Sir, please don't say I told you."

John stared at Sanjay for a minute, then sighed. "Okay, I won't mention you, but something has to be done. They cannot get away with what they have done."

"No, Sir, they should be punished, but rich people do what they like here. People like me have no power. I have a wife and two girls to look after. I cannot put them in danger."

"It's okay, Sanjay. I promise I will never mention your name. Thank you."

"Thank you, Sir."

They stood in an uncomfortable silence for a moment before Sanjay offered his hand. "I'll go, Sir?"

John shook Sanjay's hand. "Are you sure you won't have something?" Sanjay smiled and shook his head and turned toward the door. John followed him out, reaching past him to open the front door.

Sanjay paused and turned to look back at John.

"What will you do now, Sir?"

"I don't know Sanjay. I don't know. But they will be punished."

17

John sat in the dimly lit living room staring at the blank wall in front of him, a glass of gin in one hand, the news clipping in the other. He took a swig of the neat spirit, then set the glass down and examined the news clipping again.

What would he do with this information? He must go to the police, but if what Sanjay had said about the police force was true, then maybe nothing would be done. Inspector Rajiv though, he seemed like an honest man, someone who would act on the information. Perhaps he should give him the benefit of the doubt?

But if the police did nothing, what was his next step? He looked down at the photo of the grinning young man and his friends. Anger started to grow. He felt it in his gut and then in his chest. It filled his body, and he clenched his left fist, crunching the news clipping into a ball, and his jaw tightened as acid rose in the back of his throat. Those bastards, smugly thinking they can get away with anything. He had read the police report, the details of what they had done to Charlotte, the evil fuckers. Raped and beaten and her body discarded in the bushes as if it was worth nothing. No-one should get away with that. He gulped down the remainder of the gin and shook his head as it burned the back of his throat. He looked down at his watch. It was too late to do anything now, but first thing in the morning, he would pay a visit to the police.

18

A t nine the next morning, John pulled into the Police Station carpark. Charlotte's car was still there, dumped in the corner, covered in a thick layer of orange dust. All four tires were flat, and weeds were growing up and through the wheel arches. He stood for a moment staring at it, saddened by the sight of her car, abandoned, eroding, just like her memory. Straightening up, he set his jaw, checked his pocket for the news clipping and walked inside, filled with renewed determination. Once again, he was shown into the Senior Inspector's Office.

"Mr. Hayes, so good to see you again. I am so sorry about what happened to Mrs. Hayes." Senior Police Inspector Basavraj Muniappa stood and walked around his desk and took John's hand in both of his. He looked him in the eye. "I am truly sorry about your loss, Mr. Hayes. If there is anything you ever need, please do not hesitate to ask." He gestured to a chair and motioned for John to sit down.

"Manjunath." S.P.I Muniappa called out.

A constable appeared in the doorway.

"Manjunath, bring some tea and call Rajiv. Tell him to come in."

John sat and studied the man in front of him, wondering what his response was going to be when he dropped his bombshell. He decided to wait until Rajiv appeared, busying himself with small talk in the meantime.

"How is the investigation going, Inspector?"

S.P.I Muniappa sighed and leaned forward on his desk, steepling his hands in front of him. "Mr. Hayes, it's still ongoing, but you know how things are here. It takes time. It's not like your England. Your Scotland Yard." He smiled as if pleased with his reference.

John said nothing, just looked at him, not helping him out.

"Mr. Hayes, the car was never found, and the only eyewitness was your driver so we never really had much to go on."

"What about any DNA from my wife's body? I saw the report." John paused to gather his emotions, the thought of what he was about to say rekindling the grief he tried so hard to contain. "She was raped multiple times."

"I'm afraid, Mr. Hayes, there was nothing conclusive. We just don't have the resources, the testing facilities we need. But rest assured, we have our best men on the job still." He looked over John's shoulder with relief as the door opened. "Ah, Inspector Rajiv, just in time. I was just telling Mr. Hayes how I have my best men still looking into his wife's unfortunate incident."

John stood and turned as Rajiv walked in. Rajiv extended his hand, a look of profound sorrow on his face. "Mr. Hayes, I'm so sorry."

John shook his hand and nodded before sitting down again.

The constable came back with three steel cups of steaming tea on a tray and passed them out. They sat in silence for a moment, Rajiv in the chair beside John, each of them savoring the hot sweet drink.

John placed his cup on the desk and removed the news clipping from his pocket. He unfolded it and placed it on the desk in front of S.P.I Muniappa.

"I came to show you something."

Muniappa looked down at the photo and narrowed his eyes. "What's this, Mr. Hayes?"

John stabbed at the picture with his finger. "This man killed my wife."

Muniappa snorted and pushed the news clipping away before leaning back in his chair, a look of scorn clearly written on his face. His eyes flicked toward Rajiv before looking back at John. "What makes you say this, Mr. Hayes? Do you have any proof?"

Rajiv leaned forward, picked up the news clipping and studied the photograph.

John shook his head, "No."

Again, Muniappa snorted and shook his head.

Rajiv placed the photograph back on the desk and studied John. "Mr. Hayes, without any evidence, we cannot act on this information."

Muniappa held up his hand in front of Rajiv, silencing him. "You do realize who this man is? He is a prominent member of society. Very well regarded. I think it's highly unlikely he would have anything to do with such a despicable act, Mr. Hayes." He shook his head. "I know you are upset, it was a tragic thing to happen, but you can't come in here and make accusations against members of the public like this."

"I know it was him!"

"With respect, Mr. Hayes, how? You weren't even there."

John shook his head in frustration, leaning forward in his chair. He glared at Muniappa and pointed at the photo, "I know it was him! There must be something you can do? Bring him in and question him!"

Rajiv reached forward and placed his hand on John's arm. "Mr. Hayes." John sat back in his chair and turned his attention to Rajiv.

"Mr. Hayes, we want to help you, but we can't bring someone in without any form of evidence. Do you have anything at all to help back up what you are saying?"

John sighed, shook his head, and looked down at his hands.

"Then there is little we can do, Mr. Hayes, and these people, in particular, are highly connected. They will not even allow us into their house."

"But you are the police!"

Rajiv sighed and sat back in his chair and nodded. "I know."

Muniappa stood and scowled at Rajiv, "It's highly unlikely this man had anything to do with it." He extended his hand to John. "Mr. Hayes, I suggest you go home and forget about this. I know you are upset, but please don't accuse upstanding citizens of our city without anything to back you up. Good day, Mr. Hayes."

John slapped his thigh in frustration and stood. He looked at Muniappa's extended hand, then his face. Locking eyes with him, he curled his lip in disgust, then without a word, he turned on his heel and walked out, leaving Muniappa, his hand still held out, glaring angrily at Rajiv.

19

I n a repeat of the evening before, a knock at the door roused John from his alcohol-induced haze. He rubbed his face and looked at his watch. It was seven o'clock, dark outside, and just as dark inside, John not bothering to turn on the lights.

He found Inspector Rajiv standing on the doorstep, dressed in civilian clothes.

"Can I come in, Mr. Hayes?"

John stood to one side, not saying anything, and held the door open. Rajiv walked in and waited, not knowing where to go. John walked past him into the living room, switching on the overhead light and sitting down in the armchair. Rajiv followed him in, glancing at the cardboard boxes, his eyes flicking over the half-empty bottle of gin on the floor beside the chair. He sat down in the other armchair. John poured himself another drink, looking up at Rajiv questioningly.

Rajiv shook his head, "No, thank you."

John took a large mouthful of gin and swallowed, but it

was doing little to dull the feeling of helplessness. They sat in silence, John staring at the glass, Rajiv perched on the edge of his seat.

Rajiv cleared his throat. "Mr. Hayes. I know things have been extremely tough for you. I can't imagine how it feels to lose someone you love."

John said nothing, just stared at the glass in his hand.

"Mr. Hayes, can I speak off the record?"

John nodded.

"I've investigated as much as I can over the past few months, but I have come up against a brick wall." He paused, took a deep breath and continued, "I think you could be right about this man. Sunil Patil has a reputation for getting in trouble. But we don't have anything to link him to what happened."

"The car is his," John finally broke his silence.

"Yes, but the car was reported stolen."

"How convenient," John made no effort to hide the bitterness in his voice.

Rajiv sighed. "I think I will have a drink."

John gestured toward the bottle. "Help yourself, there's a glass in the kitchen."

Rajiv fetched himself a glass, reached down for the bottle, and poured a small measure of gin. He walked toward the window before taking a sip, grimacing at the unfamiliar taste, and looked out into the darkness. John watched him, studying his reflection in the window, waiting for him to continue. Rajiv looked troubled, his face a maelstrom of conflicting emotions. Rajiv took another sip of his drink, seemed to come to a decision and turned to face John.

"Mr. Hayes, I will never be able to catch the people who did this. If it is the man you say it is, he is well connected politically, his father is a senior minister in the State Government. Muniappa doesn't do anything without permission from political leaders like him. If I start sniffing around this man, you can guarantee I will be transferred out of this station within the week." He sighed, crossed the room, and sat back in the armchair.

"These people are untouchable, I'm sorry to say. It breaks my heart and goes against everything I believe in, against everything I learned in the police academy. But the reality is tough. There is no justice for people like yourself, Mr. Hayes. We live in a system ruled by the rich and powerful."

They sat in silence for a moment, the weight of Rajiv's words heavy in the room.

After a while, John spoke up, "So what do I do? Just sit back and let Charlotte's killers go free?"

Rajiv stared into his glass before draining it in one large swallow. "I'm afraid that's all you can do, Mr. Hayes. I'm really sorry." Rajiv stood and looked at John. "Mr. Hayes, please, I know it's hard, but forget this. Move on with your life. Start afresh." He looked around at the boxes. "Maybe somewhere new."

John didn't answer, didn't look at him, his eyes filled with tears. Rajiv watched him for a moment, then walked toward the door, placing his empty glass on the hall table, and let himself out.

John waited until he heard the door close, then gave in to his emotions—the tears turned to sobs, and he curled up in his chair, his body shaking with grief. He cried and cried until no more tears would come. The grief spent, the pain in his chest turned to anger. Roaring with frustration, he hurled his glass at the wall, watching it shatter into pieces, the remnants of his drink dribbling down the wall.

He couldn't let it be. He wouldn't run away like a coward. He owed it to Charlotte to make sure her attackers were punished, and if the system wouldn't do it, then maybe he had to find another way.

"I won't let you down, Charlie!"

20

John drove carefully down the rutted, muddy track which led into the Laxminagar slum. Although named for the Hindu Goddess of Wealth, somehow, she had overlooked this area when doling out her blessings. Single-story huts, made of mud brick and concrete, lined each side, separated from the track by a gutter filled with a stagnant black liquid. John slowed further as two children ran barefoot across the lane, pushing a bicycle tire with a stick. Chickens pecked vigorously in the dirt before scattering as his SUV approached. A woman in a voluminous night-dress sat in her doorway, drying her thick black hair in the sun. She looked up curiously as he passed, then went back to untangling her hair with her fingers. John looked at each house carefully. He had been down this way only once before, so he had to concentrate to find the right house. Feeling he was in the right general area, he found a small patch of open ground occupied by a mob of hungry goats grazing near the rusted shell of an abandoned rickshaw and pulled over. Getting out, he looked up and down the street before approaching a lady who was sitting in her doorway, picking stones out of a wicker basket of rice.

"Sanjay?" he asked, guessing here, everyone knew their neighbors.

The lady looked at him curiously before waving at the next hut with her free hand. "Next."

"Thank you."

She bobbed her head, smiling, and watched as John turned and walked to the small home she had indicated, followed by a group of giggling toddlers. He smiled down at them before knocking on the wooden door and waited.

The door opened with a creak, and Sanjay's wife Pournima, stood there, the look of surprise on her face swiftly replaced with a welcoming smile.

"Sir, please come." She beckoned him inside and rushed to clear a pile of folded clothes off a plastic chair while John removed his shoes at the door. "Please," she pointed at the chair. "Sanjay coming."

John walked in and sat down as Pournima picked up a battered cell phone and dialed. She had a quick conversation in the local language, the only part John understood was his name.

"Sanjay coming," she repeated before disappearing behind a curtained doorway. John could hear pots and pans being moved around and gathered it was the kitchen.

The room was small but clean, sparsely furnished with a TV on a plastic stand in one corner and a stack of plastic chairs against one wall. There was no other furniture, but beside the kitchen door, attached to the wall was a small wooden temple, faint tendrils of smoke spiraling upwards from two burning incense sticks. The room smelled of sandalwood and flowers. Another curtained doorway led to what John assumed was the single bedroom. He could just see through the partially open curtain where a tiny child slept on a blanket on the floor.

The front door opened, and Sanjay rushed in, looking worried, slightly out of breath, damp patches around his armpits and a sheen of sweat on his forehead.

"Sir, welcome to my home." Sanjay shook John's hand nervously, obviously not used to a visit from his former employer.

"One moment, Sir."

Sanjay rushed into the kitchen, and John could hear a muffled discussion with Pournima. The curtain parted, and both Sanjay and Pournima came out, their faces beaming, Pournima carrying a tray with steaming hot tea and a plate of biscuits.

"Please, Sir, have some tea." Sanjay waved Pournima forward, and John took a steel cup of tea and helped himself to a couple of biscuits. He smiled a thank you to Pournima, then turned to Sanjay,

"How are your girls?"

"Very good, Sir," he nodded enthusiastically, his face filled with joy at the thought of his daughters. He waved to the bedroom, "Geetanjali is sleeping, and Saumya is at school. Thank you, Sir."

John nodded and sipped his tea as both Sanjay and Pournima stood watching him. He looked up at Sanjay, then at Pournima before looking back at Sanjay. Sanjay seemed to understand and muttered something to Pournima who nodded, and after smiling at John, opened the front door and walked out, leaving the two of them alone.

John took another sip of the overly sweetened tea and thought about where to start. He placed the cup on the floor beside his chair and looked Sanjay in the eye.

"Sanjay, do you think you could identify the other men?"

"I'm not sure, Sir." He paced around the room. "Sir, I can describe them for you, but I did that for the police, and it didn't help."

John thought for a moment. "I have an idea Sanjay. I promise not to bother you after this, but will you at least help me identify who was involved?"

Sanjay stopped his pacing and looked down at his feet, thinking. John said nothing, giving him time as Sanjay thought it through. He reached down for his cup, sipped his tea, and finished his second biscuit.

Sanjay looked up. "You and Madam were always good to me. You paid my hospital bills, and you are still paying me now even though I don't work for you anymore." He paused and looked toward the bedroom door, before continuing, "But I am scared, Sir. Very scared." He looked down again struggling with an internal decision. He paused for a moment and then looked up with a new, determined set to his jaw. "I will help you, Sir."

21

J ohn sat in the back seat of his SUV, a white Mahindra Scorpio. It was a common car in India, and he was confident it wouldn't stand out. In his hand was his camera, fitted with a large telephoto lens, the end of which was resting on the back of the seat in front of him. He was using the Sigma 50-500 lens he had bought for a wildlife safari he took with Charlotte not long after they had arrived in India. They had visited Bandipur National Park on the border between Karnataka and Tamil Nadu and spent three days in the jungle. It had been glorious—early morning drives in the Forest Department jeep along tracks deep in the jungle, Charlotte delighting in spotting the wildlife. They had seen a lot that trip. Hundreds of Spotted Deer and their ever-present companions, the almost human-like Hanuman Langurs, seated in the trees above. They had seen elephants, and the giant Malabar Squirrel, the massive native bison called the Gaur, and myriad birdlife. It wasn't until the last morning though they saw the prize of them all. The King of the Jungle, the magnificent tiger. It was two hours into their safari drive, and they had been sitting on the side of the track for half an hour, just waiting, their guide listening to the sounds of the jungle. Years of experience had taught him how to identify the various wildlife calls, and he sat waiting for an alarm call. The jungle was filled with sound but not the sound they wanted until suddenly, the guide stiffened and sat up straight in the driver's seat.

Khyak khyak khyak... This was the call he had been waiting for, the alarm call of the Langurs. He started the jeep and quietly edged it forward up the track. Rounding a bend, they could see a group of spotted deer standing alert, all staring in one direction, into the undergrowth on the left side of the track while in the trees the troupe of Langurs called out, *khyak khyak khyak...*

They watched, nervously staring into the undergrowth until suddenly the deer scattered, and Charlotte grabbed his arm in anticipation. John readied his camera, waiting, eyes scanning the thick foliage ahead of the jeep, then the guide whispered urgently, "There, Sir!" pointing into the undergrowth.

At first, John couldn't see anything, then Charlotte gasped as it appeared, first its head, scanning the track in both directions before it moved out into the open. It was magnificent—a beautiful orange and black striped beast, its tail lazily flicking back and forth as it stopped in the middle of the track and looked back at them curiously. It had no fear—it was, after all, the King of the Jungle, comfortable in his position at the top of the food chain. Yawning lazily, it continued across the track, its giant paws padding softly in the sand before it disappeared into the jungle on the other side. Charlotte turned to John and hugged him, tears in her eyes, breathless with exhilaration. John couldn't believe what he had just seen. No nature documentary on TV could ever have prepared him for the sight of a tiger in its natural habitat. He was stunned. It was a minute or two before he realized he hadn't taken any photos.

John now sat in wait again, the object of the stakeout this time a different kind of predator. He had parked the vehicle at the end of the road, tucked behind another car and under a large Gulmohar tree. Hidden in the shade, he was confident he couldn't be spotted by his quarry. He picked up the camera, and looking through the viewfinder, he focused on the gate. The gate of Surya Patil's house.

It was a waiting game, but each time a man entered or exited the gate, he took a photo of their face, the lens at full zoom, capturing their image perfectly. He had packed a sandwich and a couple of bottles of water, expecting a long wait. Despite the shade, it was still oppressively hot inside the car, but he didn't want to run the engine and the air-conditioning for fear of attracting attention, so he wound down the windows slightly and endured the heat, glad he had chosen to wear light clothing.

The house was a hive of activity as visitors seeking favors from Surya Patil streamed in and out of the gate the whole day, and after five hours he had taken hundreds of photos. It was after seven p.m., and he was tired and hungry. The water had been finished long ago, and he had resorted to peeing in the bottle rather than leave in search of a toilet.

He was about to pack up when he saw both the gates open and a white Mercedes C Class pulled out and turned in his direction. John grabbed his camera and readied the lens while sinking down into the back seat to avoid being seen. As it passed under a street light, he was able to take a few shots of the car's occupants through the windscreen—the driver, his passenger sitting next to him, and another young man sitting in the back seat, leaning forward between the two front seats. They were all laughing at a shared joke and completely unaware of John and his car. He ducked down anyway, as the car drove past him, then peered over the back seat as he watched the Mercedes reach the end of the street and turn right.

John opened the door and moved around to the driver's seat, started the engine, and pulled out, doing a three-point turn to head after the Mercedes.

He kept his distance, hanging back as far as possible while still keeping the vehicle in sight. Fortunately, traffic going into the city was lighter at that time of the evening, and most of the traffic was in the opposite direction. He followed the car past Windsor Manor Circle and along the Golf Course Road. At the next traffic signal, he reached behind him and grabbed the camera off the back seat, placing it on the passenger seat beside him, ready for use. The Mercedes drove on past the Chinnaswamy Cricket Stadium before turning left onto M. G. Road. At the junction with Brigade Road, it turned right then shortly after, right again onto the narrower Church Street. John slowed and pulled to the side as the Mercedes pulled up outside a bar. He grabbed his camera and clicked away as the three men got out, the driver handing the keys to a valet. The men walked up the steps to the bar, greeting the doorman and slapping him on the shoulder. John checked the photos were clear, then laid the camera on the seat beside him. He wasn't exactly sure what to do next, but he felt he had enough photos to start.

22

The next morning, after a quick call to Sanjay, John was back at Sanjay's house, this time with his laptop. Pournima smiled nervously at him before preparing tea, then left the house, leaving the two men alone. John pulled up a spare plastic chair and placed his laptop on it. He had transferred the photos from his camera the night before, deleting the duplicates and unclear ones, and arranging them in order with the photos taken outside the bar in a separate folder. That was the folder he opened first.

He beckoned Sanjay to sit beside him, and Sanjay pulled his chair over and leaned forward to look at the screen. John opened the first photo of the three men exiting the Mercedes and entering the bar.

"Do you recognize these men, Sanjay?"

Sanjay looked closely, his brow furrowed in concentration. He pointed at the screen, "That is Sunil Patil. The man from the newspaper. He was there when..." he swallowed, not wanting to finish the sentence. John hastily moved to the next photo, one in which the driver and the passengers' faces were caught clearly. Sanjay narrowed his eyes and leaned closer to the screen.

"Sir, I think it was them too." He looked up at John excitedly.

John scrolled through the next couple of photos, allowing Sanjay time to examine each one.

"Yes, Sir, it was them. I am sure of it."

"Are you sure Sanjay? It was dark, remember."

"Sir, I will never forget that night. And I will never forget them. It was these men, I'm sure of it."

A look of puzzlement came across his face. "But Sir, there were four men."

"I have a lot more photos, Sanjay." John opened the folder of the photos taken outside Surya Patil's house.

"There is a lot here, Sanjay, take your time. Use the right arrow here on the keyboard to move to the next photo."

Sanjay nodded and nervously tapped the arrow key, gaining confidence as he moved through the photographs. John sat back and waited, sipping Pournima's hot sweet tea.

After a few minutes, Sanjay frowned and looked up. "How do I go back, Sir?"

"Use this left arrow."

Sanjay tapped at the keyboard and stared at the screen. "Sir, I think he is the other man."

John swiveled the screen so he could see it clearly. A group of four men was photographed walking from a jeep toward the gate. "Which one Sanjay?"

Sanjay pointed at the taller of the men, a bearded man in his twenties, with a stocky build, clad in a white *Kurta* and pajama and a large red *tilaka* mark on his forehead. "Him, Sir. Definitely him."

"Are you sure, Sanjay?"

"Yes, Sir. I'm sure. He was dressed the same way that

night. I remember his beard and his *tilaka*. He was the one who kicked me."

John nodded and sat back in the chair and looked out the small window onto the street outside, deep in thought. A cow stood in the road, staring back at him, chewing contentedly on its cud.

"What will you do now, Sir?"

"I don't know, Sanjay. I don't know. But one thing is for sure. We have already found out more than the police ever did."

23

John was obsessed. He had been watching them for a week now, parking on the street outside Surya Patil's house each day and waiting, noting what time the men arrived, what time they left, and when they did leave, he followed them. He knew where each of them lived, their favorite bars and coffee shops, what cars they drove. He made a mental note of everything but still didn't know what he would do with the information. John had no plan. He just wanted to know everything he could about Charlotte's killers and make sure, in some way, they were punished. He had canceled his return flight to England indefinitely and put his life on hold while he watched and waited. His hatred for them consumed him—their smug faces, their cocky swagger, their carefree enjoyment of life— all fueled the fire raging inside him. For them, it was as if the whole incident was a minor blip on their consciousness. They had destroyed his life, taking away forever the only person he had ever really cared about, the only person he had truly loved, and yet they carried on as if nothing had happened. He intended to make them pay, he didn't know how, but he promised himself each and every one of them was going to suffer.

By now, he had built up a profile on each of the four men. The ringleader appeared to be the one he knew as Sunil Patil, son of the politician, Surya Patil. The other three frequently met at his house and appeared to defer to him when they were out. He was in his mid-twenties, of medium height, with a build that suggested he had been a visitor to the gym at some time in the past but not that recently. His clothes were expensive casual, and his fleshy face was framed with ever-present stubble. John had never seen him before midday, his frequent late nights in the city's bars meant he never woke early.

Then there was the fat one. John didn't know his name, so he christened him Fatty. About the same age as Sunil, he was another young man whose parent's wealth ensured he never had to do a stroke of work. He lived not far from Sunil but spent most of his days at Sunil's house when they weren't out partying. He, too, had the group's uniform of three days stubble and expensive casual clothes, although his struggled to contain the rolls of fat encasing his frame.

In contrast was the skinny one he had nicknamed Bones. Taller than the rest, he was painfully thin, his clothes hanging off his bony frame. He drank more than the rest and was always fidgeting, his eyes constantly darting around. John wouldn't have been surprised if alcohol wasn't the strongest of his vices, his pale skin and eyes sunken deep in their sockets pointing toward an addiction of some sort.

Finally, there was the one he called Swami. Unlike the others, he dressed only in a white *Kurta* and pajama, the uniform of a politician trying to appear a "man of the people." He invariably had a big red *tilaka* mark on his forehead, displaying his piety to all and sundry and drove around in an Indian-made jeep, eschewing the fancy foreign cars of his friends. Swami was the only one who had a job of sorts. From what John could work out, he seemed to be involved with Sunil's father in the political party, some sort of student leader although, like the others, he was a few years past his student days. Whatever he did, it kept him busy during the day and into the early evenings, only joining the others at night.

Apart from Swami, they all lived in the same neighborhood, had access to expensive foreign cars, and had plenty of cash to spend. Fatty and Bones wouldn't surface until around midday when one by one they would appear at Sunil's house. They would hang out there or head to a coffee shop before moving on to the bars in the evenings.

John took a sip of water from the plastic bottle on the seat beside him and stretched his arms and legs. It had been a long day, and not much had happened. He was bored, hot and tired. Keeping the hours Sunil and his friends maintained had played havoc on his own sleep patterns, and sitting for hours in a hot, stuffy car didn't help. He wanted to get out and walk, to stretch properly, and to pee. To pee anywhere but in the collection of plastic bottles lying in the rear footwell. But it was almost nine-thirty at night now—the time when they usually headed into town to party—and the risk of being seen was too great.

He was sure the night would follow a similar pattern to all the others that week, but at the moment, the street and the house were quiet. John watched as a brown and white dog of indeterminate breed approached the car in front of his and sniffed the tires. John yawned and looked at his watch again—nine-thirty p.m. The dog cocked its leg and urinated on the tire before trotting across the street and curling up under a tree for the night. John rubbed his face and shifted uncomfortably in his seat.

John had watched them all week, drinking and smoking, generally obnoxious and arrogant. He had seen them laugh and tease girls, full of bravado when they were together. He hadn't once seen them alone with a woman. They seemed emotionally stunted, not capable of a normal relationship, one-on-one with the fairer sex. It was all so unfair, he thought to himself as he watched a rat appear from underneath a parked car and scurry across the street. These guys had everything—money, influence, and powerful parents. There was so much they could do with their lives, and all they did was piss it down the drain.

His thoughts were interrupted by the sight of the gate opening, and he slid down further into the back seat. The white Mercedes pulled out into the road and turned toward him as it had done many times in the past week. He slumped down enough so they couldn't see him and peered over the top of the front seats as the car passed by. All four of them were inside—Sunil driving, Swami beside him, the two opposites, Fatty and Bones in the rear—laughing at a shared joke. The car turned at the end of the street, and he opened the door and moved around to the driver's seat to follow them. He wasn't too worried about losing them. In the past week, he had become adept at following from a distance while negotiating the traffic. By now, he knew their favorite haunts, so even if he lost them, he was confident he could find them again without much difficulty.

The Mercedes drove fast, weaving in and out of the traffic, honking and flashing its lights, and John not wanting to bring attention to himself had difficulty keeping up. He followed them past the Golf Course, toward Ali Askar Cross, before turning right and past the Chinnaswamy Cricket

Stadium. Here they slowed as the road was clogged with fans attending a Cricket match, and John managed to catch up. At the traffic signal, the Mercedes turned left along MG Road before turning right. As they turned into Church Street, John realized where they were going. Their favorite bar, Roscoe's, apparently named after the owner's dog. The Mercedes stopped outside the bar, and John drove past averting his eyes and avoiding any eye contact. He found a parking space about a hundred meters up the road and continued watching them in the rear-view mirror as they handed the keys to the valet and climbed the steps, pushing a group of boys out of the way. The boys started to protest but stopped when they saw who it was.

John turned the engine off and settled in for a wait.

24

J ohn woke with a start and, dazed, looked at the dashboard clock—twelve-thirty a.m. He must have dozed off. He was sweating, his shirt damp and stuck to his body. Leaning forward, he turned on the ignition and wound down the window to let in some air. It was then he heard the shouting which had woken him.

Nothing could be seen in the street ahead, so John glanced in the rear-view mirror and noticed a group of people outside Roscoe's. By the body language and the volume, they were all obviously drunk and angry. Looking more closely, he identified Sunil and his friends standing in a semi-circle, facing a young man who was obviously distressed. Behind him stood another young man and two girls. John couldn't make out what he was saying, but judging by the body language, he looked pretty pissed off.

Sunil was sniggering while the other three stood behind him grinning. John strained to make out what the man was saying, something about "leave her alone." Sunil laughed then put his hand on the young man's chest and shoved him. The young man staggered backward, then with a roar, he rushed at Sunil as the two girls screamed. He swung his fist, but before it could make contact, Sunil lashed out with his foot and landed a kick on the young man's thigh. He stumbled and dropped to one knee. Sunil stepped forward and launched a right cross at the young man's face, knocking him to the ground. The girls screamed again, and the other young man rushed forward. Swami and Fatty stepped toward him, Fatty slipping behind him and grabbed him by the arms, turning the second man's body to face Swami. Swami punched him in the stomach. Fatty released him, and the man doubled over, gasping for breath. Swami grabbed his hair and kneed him in the face, blood spraying from his busted nose. Bones stood back, shifting one foot to the other, egging his friends on, as Sunil kicked the first man in the stomach repeatedly as he lay on the ground. The street was filled with the sound of the girls' screams and cries for help while a group of stray dogs barked constantly. The girls were holding onto each other and frantically looking around for help, but the street was empty apart from two rickshaws parked on the corner, their drivers standing beside them watching, but taking no action.

John didn't know what to do. He wanted to help them, but he was only one, and if he joined in, he himself would end up getting beaten up. John had never been in a fight before and had no idea how to handle himself. Fortunately, at that moment the scene was lit up by the headlights of a car turning onto the street, saving him from making a decision. The two bleeding men lay in the middle of the road, their girlfriends sobbing and huddled to one side. Sunil looked up at the car with a sneer, then cleared his throat and spat on the man at his feet. He gave him one more kick in the side, then beckoned to his friends to follow him. They walked toward the parked Mercedes, its front door open, the valet standing open-mouthed beside it. He held out the keys and stepped back hurriedly, in case he incurred their wrath as well. Swami slapped Sunil on the back and climbed into the car. Fatty and Bones laughed and looked back at the bodies before climbing into the back.

John watched as the Mercedes drove off. Once it had turned the corner, he opened the car door, and grabbing a plastic bottle of water from his car, he walked back to where the two young men were being helped to their feet by their girlfriends.

"Are you guys okay?"

They nodded, and John passed the water bottle to one of the girls. She pulled out a handful of tissues from her handbag, and after wetting them, wiped the blood off the young man's face. The girls were still sobbing. The driver and passenger of the car, two middle-aged men, got out and joined them.

"What happened?" they asked.

One of the girls spoke up. "Some guys wouldn't take no for an answer, and when my boyfriend stuck up for me, they beat him up."

The driver turned to the young men. "Are you guys okay? Do you need to go to the hospital?"

The man with the broken nose shook his head. "No, we will be okay." He winced as he spoke.

"Let's call the police. They can catch these guys. They won't have got far," suggested the driver.

"What's the point? The cops will just hassle us for being out late. Tell us that it's our own fault. And those guys are rich. They had a Mercedes. They will just pay off someone, and nothing will ever happen. Bastards."

John said nothing. He was reluctant to get involved or share he knew who they were.

The group waved toward the rickshaws, and they started up and drove closer.

The girl turned to John and the two men and said, "Thank you," before helping her boyfriend climb gingerly into the first rickshaw while the other couple climbed into the second. As they watched them drive off, the driver of the other car looked at John and shook his head.

"This city isn't as safe as it used to be."

"No," John agreed.

"One law for the rich, and one law for the rest of us." He shook his head again, then he and his companion walked back to their car.

John drove off, thinking about what he had just seen. It was late, no traffic on the roads. He drove automatically, deep in thought, not noticing his surroundings, his mind going back and forth over recent events.

These men were scum, they rode around spending freely, bullying people without fear of any consequences. Because there were no consequences for them. The rule of law didn't apply to them. The law could be bought and manipulated if you had the right connections and enough money. The police force lived in fear of their powerful fathers who could end a career and transfer a diligent police officer to some god-forsaken backwater to sit out the rest of their working lives. That was why no action was ever taken. That was why Charlotte's killers would never get their punishment, why John would never get his day in court, testifying against these brutal, entitled young men.

John realized he was back in Sunil's street, not sure how he got there. He drove slowly toward Sunil's gate and glanced over at the house. Some lights were still on but the gate was closed, and there was no sign of any watchman or security. John pulled to the side and parked, not sure what he was doing there, still disturbed about what he had seen outside the bar. Part of him felt ashamed he hadn't done anything, he had just sat there and watched. How was he different from everyone else then? Perhaps he should have helped, but he knew, in the big picture, it wouldn't stop their behavior. It certainly wouldn't have helped get justice for Charlotte. Closing his eyes, he pictured Charlotte smiling at him.

"Charlotte, I'm doing this for you. I will make sure these animals are punished for what they did to you." He paused for a minute, trying hard to create a clear vision of her in his mind's eye. It was getting harder and harder to picture Charlotte clearly, and it made him feel guilty. "I'm sorry Charlotte. I miss you so much." Her image faded and he sighed.

Opening his eyes, he reached forward to turn the ignition key and stopped, his fingers still on the key, as he watched Sunil's gate open and Bones stumble out. His gait was unsteady, the effects of the night's alcohol consumption glaringly evident. John had followed Bones home before, so he knew where he lived. Like all the group, he too lived with his parents, their house just two streets away. It was a short walk when sober, but Bones was far from sober. John watched as he stumbled on an uneven paving slab but regained his footing. He looked around and decided to walk down the center of the road, it was smoother and easier to navigate in his inebriated state. The dog sleeping at the foot of the tree looked at him quizzically, but seeing no threat, tucked its head back down into its belly and went back to sleep. John started the engine and without turning on the lights, pulled smoothly out into the road and crept after him, keeping his distance. Bones reached the end of the street and stopped, looking both ways, trying to remember his way home before deciding on left. John turned after him and wound down his window. He could hear Bones talking to himself as he weaved his way down the street. Bones paused beside a parked Toyota Innova, muttering to himself and unzipped his pants. John stopped the car and watched as he peed on the back tire like a dog marking its territory. Swaying back and forth, his urine splashed the tire, the road, and his shoes. He tried to zip himself up but gave up. Instead, he reached into his back pocket and pulled out a hip flask, took a swig and staggered a few feet further down the road. John followed him and increased his speed. He got closer, not sure what he was doing. It was as if something else had taken control of his body. Bones, for the first time, heard the engine and turned to look back in John's direction. John switched on his headlights, flicking them to full beam and pressed his foot a little harder on the accelerator. Bones, blinded by the headlights, held up his hand as if to tell John to stop and made to move to one side, but he was too drunk to be able to find a gap between the parked vehicles to get off the road. He stumbled forward.

"Wait, wait," he slurred, one hand held up in the air the other clutching his hip flask. John closed the distance, then slowed to match his speed as Bones, now in a panic, started to jog. Just a couple of meters behind him John followed, Bones staggering in front of him, his drunken state causing him to swerve from side to side.

John chased him like this down the street, pushing him along, watching his spindly bony legs carry him as fast as his drunken state would carry him. He was muttering to himself, part of him understanding he needed to get out of the way, but not fully comprehending the danger he was in.

John felt strangely detached from the scene unfolding in front of him. It was like watching on television a predator chasing its prey to exhaustion. Bones took a right turn at the end of the street, John still following him closely. They weren't going fast, a little more than a slow jog. He could at any time have ducked between the cars and got out of the way, but his brain wasn't working. His legs were getting tired, and he stumbled, his chest rising and falling with exertion.

John was right behind him, and he revved the engine, the sound prompting Bones to attempt a burst of speed. He looked back at John, his eyes wide with fear, and as he did so his toe caught the edge of a pothole, and he fell flat on the road. It happened so fast, John didn't have enough time to react. He stomped his foot on the brake pedal, but it was too late, and with a sickening thud, he felt the front left tire run over his body, followed by one more thud as the back tire rode over him as well. John stopped the vehicle and stared straight ahead. What had he done? His heart pounded in his chest, and with a shaking hand, he opened the door. He stepped out and moved hesitantly toward the rear of the car, afraid of what he might see.

John saw the legs first, the right leg spread out, the left leg bent back. He ran his eyes up the rest of the body which in the dark, at first, looked okay, as if Bones was asleep on the road. His arms were askew, but the rest of his body was serene. John stepped closer and crouched down. He couldn't see if he was breathing.

"Hey, are you ok?"

There was no reply. John took a deep breath and with both hands grabbed Bones by the left shoulder and turned him onto his back.

"Oh shit! Fuck fuck fuck!" John stood up and stepped away from the body. He looked down in horror. Bones' chest was crushed with the full weight of a two-ton SUV. He was thin, to begin with, but the weight of the car had crushed his ribs like matchsticks. John looked around to see if anyone was watching. There was no one around.

"What do I do, what do I do?" he paced back and forth. "Fuck!" John walked back to the body and crouched down. Bones' mouth was open, and a trickle of blood ran from both nostrils down the side of his face. His eyes bulged from the sockets, wide open and staring straight at him. He was definitely dead. John stood, took a deep breath, and looked around. The street was empty and poorly lit, no signs of light from any of the houses. Bones' hip flask lay in the middle of the road where it had fallen.

There was nothing he could do for him now, and anyway, how would he explain what had happened? Why had he chased him? He was so fucking stupid! He stepped away from the corpse, his whole body shaking now. Shit, shit, shit. He had to get out of there. He ran around to the front of the car and climbed back in, the engine still running. Slipping it into gear, he pulled away quietly, not wanting to arouse anyone. As he neared the end of the street, he looked back in his rear-view mirror. He could just make out the shape of the body lying in the road, just beyond the light cast by the nearest streetlamp. Three stray dogs approached it warily, sniffing it with interest before looking up the road in John's direction. John turned the corner and sped away.

25

When John reached his home, sleep was the last thing on his mind. Adrenaline, fear, and guilt coursed through his body. He grabbed a bottle of gin from the kitchen cupboard, removed the cap, and took a long swig from the bottle, gulping it down without tasting it, then took another swig. Placing the bottle on the kitchen countertop, he paced back and forth, unable to settle down. What had he done? He had just taken a man's life. No matter how reprehensible the man, he had no right to take his life. He was no better than these men he despised. He shook his head. He was a murderer!

John grabbed the bottle and took another large mouthful, the liquid burning his throat and filling his chest with warmth, the alcohol starting to calm his nerves a little. He walked into the living room and collapsed into the armchair, bottle in hand. What would happen now? He was now a criminal. He put the bottle down on the floor beside him and looked at his hands, still shaking. He needed to calm down. He picked up the bottle, took another large mouthful, gulping it down, then stood and walked back to the kitchen. He ran the kitchen tap and splashed cold water over his face, then grabbed the liquid dish soap, pouring it over his hands and rubbing them together under the flowing water, working up the suds, scrubbing them hard. His hands were already clean, but this symbolic act seemed to work deeper, cleansing him of what had happened and calming him down. Turning off the tap he leaned on the kitchen counter and stared out the window into the darkness of the back garden.

A clear vision of Charlotte leaped into his mind, her gentle laugh as she stood barefoot on the lawn, the sun streaming through her long golden hair. A tear ran down his cheek as he remembered their times together. Times that would no longer be repeated, times that had so violently been taken away from him. The guilt subsided, replaced by a feeling of satisfaction. Bones got what he deserved. He had taken Charlotte's life, now John had taken his. An eye for an eye—that's what it was. John had done the right thing. Bones would never have been punished by the legal system and would have continued living his life, happily drinking and partying and treating people like shit. Bones got what he deserved, and John was the one who gave it to him. He straightened up, filled with a new resolve.

"For you Charlotte," he said out loud. "For you."

John woke late, his temples throbbing, his head heavy with a hangover. As his eyes opened, the events of the night before came rushing back. Jumping out of bed, he rushed downstairs, opened the front door, and ran outside to look at the car. The front was unmarked, no dents or scratches. He bent down to examine the tires, first the front, then walked back, bending down to inspect the rear tires. There was no sign anything had happened. He straightened up and breathed a sigh of relief as Mr. Reddy from two doors down walked past with his Alsatian, a large stick in his hand. He raised the stick in greeting, looking quizzically at John, and John realized he was still standing in his boxer shorts and t-shirt. He returned the greeting and went back inside.

John scooped a measure of coffee beans into his grinder and switched it on, grinding them into a powder before tipping it into the French press. He poured boiling water over the coffee powder and waited while it brewed, staring out the window over the back garden. There was no sign of any damage to his car, and apart from a stray dog or two, no one had seen what had happened. Had he just committed the perfect crime? No-one could link him to the victim. It didn't even look like a murder. The victim was drunk, fell asleep on the road, then hit by an unknown vehicle. Happened all over the city. Case closed.

But what did that make John? A murderer? Yes. But did Bones deserve it? Yes. So, that made John an avenger, a vigilante, a modern-day Charles Bronson. He had two options. He could sit around and wait for the police to take action—which was never going to happen, he would die of old age before these guys were punished—or he could take matters into his own hands. He could do to the others what he had done to Bones. Any time he had any doubts he just had to look at the police reports and see what those bastards had done to his Charlotte. He was no longer sad and bitter, he was determined. Finally, he saw a way forward, and he felt calm for the first time in months.

John pushed down the plunger on the French press and poured himself a cup of coffee. Picking up the mug in both hands, he sipped the hot, bitter brew. He knew what he had to do. He just didn't know how.

26

J ohn didn't go back to Sunil's house for a few days, thinking it prudent to lie low for a while before returning. There hadn't been much in the news about Bones. Nothing on the TV, just a brief report in the local paper. *"Anil Goswami, only son of prominent industrialist Deepak Goswami, died yesterday..."* Very brief and nothing about how it had happened. John presumed the "prominent industrialist" didn't want stories of his no-good son's drunken partying lifestyle to be plastered all over the newspapers. It suited John. He was sure the police would fail to follow up. They were far too understaffed and unmotivated to find out which car in a city of eight million people had run over a drunkard sleeping in the road at night. Now, he had to concentrate on the other three. His time spent observing them had established patterns—he knew where they lived and how they spent their time. He didn't yet know how to use the information to his advantage, so he spent his time thinking, running over scenarios in his mind, thinking of ways in which he could kill them and get away with it. He remembered movies, books he had read, anything to give him an idea. Nothing much really helped. After three days, he still was no closer to a solution.

So, John decided to go back and watch them. Maybe, just maybe, the universe would present him with an opportunity—just as it had done with that no-good son of a bitch, Anil, and his skinny ass.

So, on the fourth day of the new John—vigilante John, avenging angel John—he once again found himself sitting in the back seat of his SUV, parked in the shade of the one-hundred-year-old Gulmohar tree, bottles of water on the seat beside him, a packet of sandwiches on his lap—watching, waiting.

John had changed, but the street was the same. Big luxurious houses on each side, the road lined with ancient shade trees—Flame of the Forest, Jacaranda, and Gulmohar. The pack of stray dogs at John's end of the street hovered around, stretching and yawning, occasionally casting a wary eye toward the pack of stray dogs that occupied the other end of the street. A koel called from the tree above, its cuckoo-like sound rising above the background cawing of crows and cooing of pigeons. It was an idyllic scene with no hint of John's intent. Now and then, a gate would open, and a gardener or watchman would dump a bucket full of garden waste in the gutter, often sending a long stream of red tobacco spittle after it. Servants would come and go, the maids in colored saris, the gardeners in their suit pants and vests. Outside Sunil's house, the elderly watchman sat on his plastic chair, one leg tucked up underneath him, one sandal lying on the ground below. He would occasionally shout out a greeting to the watchman of another house or pass a lewd comment as a maid scurried past, often inviting a stream of invective in return. By mid-morning, activity at the house increased, as it usually did whenever Surya Patil was in town, with a stream of people coming in and out of the gate, clutching papers and files, all vying for a piece of his attention as he wielded his political power and took his chunk of flesh in exchange for granting favors.

As John sat and observed the rhythm of the street, he thought about the three men. He wanted to keep Sunil Rao until last. He was the group leader, they all looked up to him and wouldn't do anything without his approval. John wanted him to wonder what was happening, to be frightened, worried about when the Grim Reaper would be coming for him. And John wanted him to suffer—no random car accident for him.

Swami would be difficult. He always seemed to be surrounded by party workers, John rarely saw him alone. It would take careful planning and thought. No, Fatty would be the next one.

Fatty... John still didn't know his real name, but Fatty suited him. He was about two hundred fifty pounds of blubber, unfit, soft, no doubt spoilt by his indulgent parents from a young age. John knew where he lived, just four streets away in the same suburb, but he spent most of his time at Sunil's house or out partying with him. The only time he was alone was on his thrice-weekly visit to the local branch of Gold's Gym. John had watched him from outside as he seemed to spend his whole-time walking on one of the treadmills set up in the large floor-to-ceiling windows overlooking the street. The amount of energy he expended, plodding away, sweating like a pig in his fancy tracksuit was never going to be enough to counterbalance his eating habits. He was a glutton, constantly stuffing his face with chips, deep-fried snacks from the street vendors, and when out with Sunil, copious amounts of beer.

An idea began to form. Maybe that was how John would

get him. He could poison him. Make him choke on his favorite food and die face down in his plate. That would be a fitting end to the fat fucker.

It sounded simple enough, but it presented John with another problem. Poison him with what and how to administer it without getting caught? He needed to research. John climbed back into the front of the Scorpio and started the engine. No sense wasting time watching the house, he had work to do.

27

Back home, he brewed himself a fresh pot of coffee and opened his laptop on the kitchen counter. The first thing that sprang to mind was rat poison. It was readily available in any local grocery or household goods store. Could he add it to food? Did it have a taste? How much to dose him with and how long would it take to work? Opening his browser John typed in, "Can a person die eating rat poison?" Judging by the search results, he wasn't the first to ask this question. How many people are out there trying to kill others with rat poison? Perhaps he should start a club? They could compare notes. John made a mental note to destroy his hard drive once this was all over.

He spent a couple of hours, and two pots of coffee, burrowing down the internet rabbit hole, researching rat poison and alternatives. But he kept going back to one thing. How would he administer it without getting caught?

Whatever he used, it needed to be odorless, tasteless, and easily administered. Perhaps with a syringe? He could walk past his table in a restaurant and squirt it into his food. No. Too risky. He would be seen by someone. Perhaps he could jab him when he goes to the toilet? But then it would need to be fast acting because he would know who had done it and would tell someone. No, there had to be an easier way. John needed to think.

He closed his laptop and sat back, rubbing his face with his hands. He was looking at this too closely. He needed to take a step back, clear his head, and let the idea come on its own. He stood and walked to the back door, opened it, and stepped out into the back garden.

The heat of the day was oppressive in most places, but here in the garden with the shade from the trees around the border, it was quite pleasant. John walked into the middle of the lawn, the grass struggling to survive in the summer heat. He had not watered it for days, his mind occupied with more important things. He took a deep breath and closed his eyes, clearing his head. In the trees above him, a pair of mynahs squabbled, and further away, the strident call of a koel broke the silence. Opening his eyes, he paced toward the end of the garden and back again, his eyes running over the foliage but not really seeing. High above in the sky, birds of prey soared in the blue expanse, and in the distance, the sound from the highway, honking and lorry engines, carried gently in the breeze.

The rat poison idea worried him. There was none in the house, he would have to buy some, and that would mean he could always be identified. The number of foreign people going into a local shop to buy rat poison would be few and far between which would mean any shopkeeper would remember him. The same would go for any other form of readily available poison. During his time in India, he had often read in the news of people committing suicide by drinking pesticides or floor cleaner, but these were still things that had to be purchased. It was all too risky. As hell-bent as he was for revenge, he didn't want to get caught. Spending the rest of his life in an Indian prison was not part of the plan.

The cooing of a pigeon interrupted his thoughts, and he looked up to where it was seated on a branch, looking down at him. A pair of bulbuls flitted from branch to branch, and from the corner of his eye, he spotted the movement of a squirrel jumping from one tree to another. He watched as it raced up a long branch and paused in the fork. It had something in its paw, and it stopped to nibble on it. John had an idea.

He rushed back into the house and opened up the laptop again and typed in, "Poisonous plants of India."

The search results presented him with a number of options. There was Datura which had poisonous seeds and flowers. It was often used in suicide, but the level of toxicity varied wildly from plant to plant. The castor oil plant which grew wild everywhere and whose seeds contained the deadly toxin, Ricin. There was Yellow Oleander of which most parts were poisonous. And then a name caught his eye. "The Suicide Tree."

His interest piqued, he read further. *Cerbera Odollam,* or as it is locally known, "The Pong Pong Tree," grows wild along the coasts of southern India. According to the Wikipedia entry, it was dubbed the "suicide tree" as it was found to be responsible for a huge number of poisonings, both for suicide and homicide. The seeds contain a highly toxic glycoside called *cerberin*, just one seed being enough to induce death in an adult. In small doses, the toxin would induce stomach pain, vomiting, and diarrhea. In large enough doses, it would stop a person's heart. It worked within hours of ingestion, John read. One scientist said the seeds when powdered and added to spicy food or mixed with sugar were undetectable. If the doctors did not know what the patient had ingested, *Cerbera* poisoning was extremely hard to detect and treat. The same article mentioned that the substance was difficult to detect in autopsies too, making it the perfect murder poison. After printing out a photo of the tree and its fruit, John deleted his search history and sat back in his chair. He had found the means, now he had to work out the method. But first, he had to make a trip to the seaside.

28

The journey from Bangalore to the Kerala coast by road is around three hundred kms. With the traffic congestion getting out of Bangalore and the poor condition of many of the roads, it would take John seven to eight hours of constant driving. To avoid the worst of the traffic, he left early the next morning after packing sandwiches, a flask of coffee, and six cans of Red Bull. There were places to stop en route for food, and he should really spend the night in Kerala before heading back, but he didn't want to risk anyone linking him to the route at a later date. John wanted no record of a hotel stay—all hotels in India requiring a form of ID before checking guests in—so that was too risky. And he didn't want anyone in a roadside *dhaba* to remember a foreigner stopping for coffee and a meal. For the same reason, he left his phone switched on and at home, having read somewhere a person's movements could be tracked both in real time and retrospectively by monitoring their phone's connections as it roamed between cell phone towers. If anyone checked on him, it would show he had been at home the whole day.

At five a.m., there wasn't much traffic on the roads, so he drove straight through the center of Bangalore, the streets seeming so wide and empty, a rare sight in a city which was expanding faster than the infrastructure could cope. He marveled at the giant old trees lining the sides of the roads and wondered at the foresight of the person who had the sense to plant them over a century ago, ensuring the streets would be shaded and the air to some extent purified by the green lungs of the trees.

Within forty minutes, he had crossed the city and headed south-west along the dual carriageway toward Mysore. Traffic was starting to build up but thankfully, mostly in the opposite direction with lorries laden with vegetables and coconuts heading into the markets of Bangalore. John managed to keep up a good speed along the highway for the most part but had to slow through the villages as farmers started their day, heading to their fields on tractors or slow-moving bullock carts. He reached Mysore after three hours and stopped on the ring-road to top up the fuel tank and stretch his legs, paying cash for the diesel. He wanted to avoid filling up in Kerala. If it came to it, a trip to Mysore would be easier to explain than a trip to Kerala.

Setting off again, he continued along the ring-road which skirted Mysore toward Hunsur, then followed the smooth, wide road toward the coffee growing district of Coorg where he and Charlotte had spent many lovely weekends in home-stays on the coffee estates. The plantations were lush and heavily forested, and the food, especially the famous *pandi* curry, a spicy pork curry, was delicious. It was a beautiful part of Southern India but one he felt he would never bring himself to enjoy again.

Just over two hours later, the road entered the Brahmagiri Forest, and he slowed, winding down his window and switching off the air-conditioning to savor the cool forest air. Spotted deer grazed by the roadside, and a troupe of black-faced Hanuman Langur sat on their haunches nearby, watching the traffic while others squatted high on tree branches above. Wherever he looked though, he was reminded of trips he had taken with Charlotte, the beauty of the countryside no longer filling him with wonder but instead, with sorrow. They had spent so many weekends exploring these parts of Southern India, marveling at the wildlife, the beautiful scenery, and the delicious local food. It now held little appeal for him, instead bringing back memories of what he had lost. Memories which spurred him on in his quest for vengeance.

Leaving the forest behind, the road crossed the border from Karnataka into Kerala. He passed through the check-point with ease, the Border Police, busy checking the papers of a lorry, had no interest in stopping a private car. They would no doubt insist on being given 'chai money' to smooth the process.

From the border crossing to the coastal town of Kannur took another hour and a half, the roads narrow and wind-ing, so it was around midday by the time he arrived. He bypassed the town and followed the signs leading toward the Kannur Fort and pulled into the carpark. John got out and stretched, twisting from side to side, loosening up his back and hips from the stiffness from the seven-hour drive. He found a bench, and with his flask of coffee and sand-wiches, sat down for lunch.

According to John's research the "Suicide Tree" grew along the coast, so after finishing his lunch, he drove south along the road toward the village of Eddakad. This part of Kerala was populated with small villages and settlements everywhere, but it was also heavily forested, the area filled with coconut palms, jackfruit, and mango trees. After three or four kilometers, he took a small lane on the right which led toward the beach. It was narrow, not much wider than a vehicle's width and lined with ancient, moss-covered stone walls. Here and there, a village house appeared in the shade of the trees, children playing in the packed-earth front yards, chickens foraging in the undergrowth.

John drove slowly, his eyes scanning the foliage until close to the beach, he found an area devoid of habitation. He parked the car and got out, removing the printouts from his pocket. Looking around to make sure he wasn't being observed, John stepped off the road and into the trees. The area was lush green and cool, the branches overhead filled with bird life. He wandered further from the road, brushing the branches away from his face, clearing spider webs with his hands, all the time examining each plant to find the one he needed. He knew roughly what it looked like, the tree bearing a similar resemblance to the Frangipani trees that were in his back garden. He found a trail and followed it as it wound its way between the trees heading toward the shoreline. After about a hundred meters, the trail led down to an area of mangroves, and it was there he found what he was looking for.

There was more than one tree, most of them tall with their branches too high up, but he found a smaller, younger tree, its branches hanging within reach. Its thick, green leaves were interspersed with the pretty, white, five-petaled flowers, giving no indication of the deadly toxins contained in its seeds. The fruit looked like a small, green mango. Removing his pocket knife from his back pocket, he reached up, pulled down a branch and cut off several of the fruit, placing them in a plastic bag he had brought along for the purpose.

John looked around to make sure he was unobserved, but there was no one, just the sound of insects buzzing, a family of crows in the branches overhead, and in the distance, a dog barking. He returned to the car and stowed the plastic bag filled with fruit inside a sports bag and covered it with a towel. Climbing back into the front of the car he made a U-turn for the seven-hour journey back to Bangalore.

29

S unil, Swami, and Fatty sat around a table filled with empty bottles of Kingfisher and a half-full bottle of vodka on the roof terrace of Sunil's house. The mood that evening was somber, none of the usual laughter and banter that accompanied them whenever they got together. Sunil leaned forward and stubbed out a cigarette in the overflowing ashtray as a cool breeze stirred the leaves of the tropical plants lining the seating area and rippled the canvas awning overhead.

"I can't believe it," scowled Swami. "What the fuck was he doing sleeping on the road?"

Fatty remained silent, his attention on the platter of tandoori chicken in his lap.

Sunil lit another cigarette and blew a cloud of smoke into the air. He drank directly from the bottle of vodka before replying, "If I ever find the fucker who ran him over, I'll break his legs."

Swami sneered, "Yeah right. In this city? Fat chance of finding anyone. Bro, his time was up. He was drinking himself to death, anyway, and the amount of coke he snorted that night, I'm surprised he made it as far as he did."

Sunil nodded and took another mouthful of vodka before passing the bottle to Fatty. "I should have let him stay here, but you know what my father is like. He never could stand him."

Fatty spat a chicken bone on the floor, wiped his mouth on his sleeve and took a swig of vodka, gulping it down before passing the bottle on to Swami.

Sunil stood and paced to the edge of the roof terrace, looking out across the rooftops while he finished his cigarette. He flicked the spent butt over the wall and turned to face his two friends, sitting morosely in their chairs.

"Fuck it. Drink up. You think Anil would want us to sit here feeling sorry for him? No. If it was one of us, he would be high as a kite by now." He walked back to the table and slapped Fatty on the shoulder. "Come on, Manish, get your fat ass out of the chair. Let's go into town and give Anil the send-off he deserves."

Swami smirked. "Yeah, Manish, about time you moved your butt. Let's go."

30

It was after midnight by the time John returned from Kerala and collapsed into bed, exhausted from the long drive in heavy traffic. The effects of the coffee and the Red Bull had long since worn off, and toward the end of the journey, he could barely keep his eyes open. As he drifted off to sleep, images of the journey flashed before his mind's eye, his body still feeling like it was in motion.

Nine hours later, he dragged himself out of bed and stood in the shower, alternating hot and cold water until he felt fresh again. In one of the boxes in Charlotte's studio, John found a pair of latex gloves she used to protect her hands while painting and took them downstairs. He spread a sheet of newspaper on the kitchen countertop, then put on the gloves. From the plastic bag, he removed the fruit and with a knife, cut the flesh away from the kernels and set it to one side. He wasn't sure what to do next but assumed he would need to powder them if he wanted to add it to Fatty's food. He took the seeds, three in total, arranged them on an oven tray, turned the oven on low, and placed the tray inside to dry the seeds out. An hour later he removed them and left them to cool. Once they had reached room temperature, he fetched a hammer from his toolbox and took the seeds outside. He wrapped the seeds in a cloth and placed the bundle on a sheet of newspaper laid on the garden path. With the hammer, he pounded the cloth bundle until he was sure the seeds inside were smashed into pieces, then took the cloth with the seed fragments back into the kitchen where he emptied them into the food processor. The machine made a terrible noise as the fragments bounced around inside, but the noise soon reduced to a hum as the pieces became a powder. John smelt burning from the motor, but he wasn't worried, having no intention of using it again after grinding down the toxic seeds. He scooped the resulting powder into a plastic container and fastened the lid tight before taking the food processor outside and destroying it with the hammer. He was throwing it out and wanted to make sure there was no chance an enterprising rubbish collector would attempt to recycle it. Charlotte's killers were enough to have on his conscience without adding any more innocent victims. In a black plastic rubbish bag, he gathered the pieces of the smashed blender together with the spoon, the gloves, and the kitchen cloth and kept it to one side to be discarded later on a rubbish heap on the other side of the city.

L ate the next morning, a Wednesday, he followed Fatty as he was driven the one kilometer from his home to the gym where the driver double-parked outside the entrance. He continued watching from his position a few cars back as Fatty climbed out of the Toyota Land Cruiser, slung a sports bag over his shoulder, and took a sports drink bottle from his driver. He then turned and walked toward the entrance, shaking the bottle before taking a sip. John remained in the car. There wasn't much point in him going to the gym as well and risk being spotted. In fact, after five minutes, he could see Fatty walking on one of the treadmills lined up in the window. John shook his head. The stupid fat slob would never lose weight if he gets driven to the gym to walk on a treadmill.

Just over an hour later, John watched the Land Cruiser pull up again outside the gym, double-parking and blocking one lane of the already narrow road. The cars behind honked furiously, but the driver ignored them and sat with the engine running, his arm hanging out the window. Fatty emerged from the gym door and called out to the driver who jumped out of the SUV and jogged up the steps, following Fatty back inside. Two minutes later, he came out carrying Fatty's bag, his bottle, and a large plastic container under one arm. Fatty followed behind, scrolling through his phone, his face red, big patches of sweat around his armpits and across his belly. Watching them, John had a nagging feeling he was missing something important. He concentrated as the driver switched the plastic container to his other arm, wedging it against his body and opened the rear passenger door of the Land Cruiser with his spare hand. He stood aside while Fatty hauled himself in, the vehicle visibly sagging with his weight. The driver closed the door then turned, walked to the rear, and opened the tailgate to stow the sports bag, container, and bottle. A light bulb went off in John's head, and he reached for his camera.

I n a sporting goods shop across town, John purchased a two kg container of chocolate flavored whey protein, exactly the same brand and flavor the driver had stowed in the back of the Land-Cruiser. He added a pair of workout gloves, tracksuit pants, a t-shirt, and a generic blue drinks bottle with a wide screw-top lid. John had carefully examined the photos he had taken outside the gym, and the bottle had been easy to match. Paying cash for the items, he returned to the car and headed back home.

31

John waited in the car outside the gym, dressed in the sports gear he had purchased, a pair of workout gloves on his hands, and beside him on the seat, a hand towel and the blue plastic drinks bottle.

It was midday on a Friday, one of the three days Fatty usually came to the gym. John had called the gym the day before and told them he was thinking of joining. The enthusiastic girl on the phone had told him he was free to come anytime for a trial class.

Another fifteen minutes passed before the white Land Cruiser pulled up and double-parked at the entrance, setting off a chorus of horns from the cars held up behind it. Fatty climbed out of the back seat, slung his bag over his shoulder, blue drink bottle in his right hand, and pushed the door closed. His driver pulled away, and Fatty lumbered up the steps toward the gym.

John waited five minutes and followed. He pushed the double glass doors open, walked into the reception, and looked around. On one side was a waiting area with a black vinyl sofa and a potted fern. Several copies of bodybuilding magazines lay on a side table. Loud music boomed from a set of doors on the right which led into the workout space, and at the back of the room facing the door was the reception counter behind which sat a young girl in her early twenties. She stood up and greeted him with a big smile.

"Hello."

"Hi, are you Annamika?"

"Yes, I am, how can I help you?"

"My name is Paul, I called yesterday about coming to try out the gym."

"Yes, Mr. Paul. Let me show you around."

Annamika came around the counter, still smiling. She was a pretty girl, dressed in a tracksuit, her hair pulled back in a high ponytail. John followed her through the doors into the main equipment floor and scanned the room, looking to see how many people were there and where Fatty had gone. A line of treadmills faced the plate-glass windows overlooking the street, and of the five machines, three were occupied. Fatty was already plodding away on the furthest one from the entrance. The one next to him was empty while the next couple were occupied by two teenage girls, clad in brightly colored workout clothing, their faces fully made up as if they were at a party. They chatted away to each other as they walked, barely breaking a sweat.

Next to the treadmills, a selection of weight machines filled the center of the room, and behind them, along the mirrored rear wall, stood a rack of free weights. The gym was empty apart from a skinny young man examining the size of his biceps in the mirror and a trainer sitting in the corner on an unused bench press, scrolling through his phone.

"Have you used a gym before, Mr. Paul? If not, I can ask Rahul to guide you around the machines." She gestured toward the guy on the phone who looked up at the sound of his name. Seeing nothing of interest, he went back to his phone.

John smiled at her and shook his head, "No thank you, I'm quite familiar with all these machines. I have used them before."

"Awesome." She waved toward another set of doors. "The changing rooms are in there. You can leave your bag in one of the lockers. When you have finished, come and see me about membership."

John returned her smile and nodded. He looked around the room again, his eyes scanning the treadmills, careful not to catch Fatty's eye. Fatty was still staring out the window as he labored away on the treadmill, his water bottle in the cup holder at the front of the machine. John walked into the men's changing room and removed his phone, towel, and the water bottle before placing the bag inside the locker, not bothering to lock it as he planned to leave quickly. With the towel, he wiped the water bottle one more time. He was wearing the workout gloves but wanted to make doubly sure there were no fingerprints. He took a deep breath and walked out into the gym.

Picking the furthest treadmill from Fatty, he looped the towel over the handrail, placed the water bottle and his phone in the cup holder and started the machine. From his previous observations, he knew that Fatty spent around thirty minutes walking on the treadmill before moving to the weight machines. John estimated fifteen minutes had passed since he started, so in another fifteen minutes, he would make his move. His stomach churned with nerves, and he increased the speed of the treadmill, running faster in an effort to stay calm, the two girls beside him still strolling along as if they were walking in the mall.

Fifteen minutes later, Fatty turned off his treadmill and stepped off the machine. John watched him in the reflection as he picked up his bottle, gave it a shake and took a large mouthful before mopping the sweat from his face with a towel. His shirt was soaked through, rolls of fat visible through the now transparent cloth sticking to his body, and his chest heaved with exertion. He looked like a heart attack waiting to happen. That suited John perfectly.

Fatty moved to the seated press, set his bottle to the side, and put the pin through the second plate before starting his reps. With only ten kilograms on the stack, John thought it unlikely Fatty would ever lose any weight. Anyway, weight loss would soon be the least of Fatty's worries.

John continued to run for a couple more minutes, then slowed the treadmill to a walking pace, watching Fatty perform another lethargic set on the seated press. John counted out the reps in his head. He had seen Fatty do ten reps the last set, and as Fatty reached eight reps, John stopped the treadmill and stepped off. He turned on a countdown alarm for five minutes on his phone, grabbed the towel, and the bottle and walked toward the weight machines just as Fatty stood up. John approached him as if to use the next machine and as he passed, he shoulder barged Fatty, knocking the drink bottle from Fatty's hand.

"Hey bro, what's your problem?" he complained. He spoke English with a slight American accent. John called it the MTV accent, many of the young staff in his office speaking the same way, fed on a diet of American television and movies.

"I'm so sorry," John replied. Keeping himself between Fatty and the water bottle lying on the floor, he bent down to pick it up with his right hand. He turned and smiled. "I didn't see you there. Here you go." John handed Fatty the bottle from his left hand.

Fatty glared and snatched the bottle before moving toward another machine. John breathed out, expelling the tension. He was halfway there. He walked to the bench press machine, set up a suitable weight and lay down on his back and started to press. After ten reps, he sat up, looking casually around the room, waiting, his eyes finding Fatty attempting a chest exercise on another machine.

The alarm rang on John's phone, and he immediately silenced it and held it to his ear. "Yes? Okay. Now? Okay, I will be there in fifteen minutes." John stood and with a glance toward the scowling Fatty, he walked toward the changing room where he retrieved his bag from the locker. Annamika looked up in surprise as he walked out into the reception.

"Mr. Paul, leaving already?"

"I'm sorry, something has come up," John pointed at the phone in his hand. "I will call you later about joining."

"Okay, Mr. Paul. We can do you a good deal," she smiled.

John smiled back, then walked outside looking left and right before dashing through a gap in the traffic to his car parked on the opposite side of the road. He threw his bag on the passenger seat, started the engine, and pulled out into the flow of traffic. He wanted to be far away before Fatty drank too much.

32

M anish Nayak, the obese young man John knew of as 'Fatty,' sat in the 'pec deck' machine. The foreigner had irritated him. These whites come into the country and think they own the place, he thought. Just like the British did before. Nothing had changed. He glanced up at the bank of TV screens above the treadmills where a music video was playing, the scantily clad, white singer pouting suggestively at the camera. Their women were alright though. Easier than these stuck up Indian girls. He looked over at the two girls who had finished on the treadmills and were dabbing the perspiration from their faces with matching pink hand towels. They gave him a dirty look, said something to each other, and burst out laughing.

"Bitches," he thought to himself. Looking away, he reached down for his bottle and took a large swig. He screwed up his face at the slightly bitter taste of the protein shake. He shook it again and took another sip. It wasn't usually that bitter. He would have to have a word with Sujata, the maid. She obviously wasn't mixing it properly.

Useless villager. It was so hard to get the servants to do their jobs properly these days. They come from their village and don't know how to do anything. No-one wants to work. He shook his head and took another sip from the bottle, then dabbed at his forehead with his hand towel. She had a nice body though.

A vision formed in his head of her bending down to mop the floor, the drape of her sari slipping away so he could see her midriff and her blouse underneath. He felt a stirring in his groin. Maybe one day he would get her alone and teach her a lesson. Show her how it's done in the city. It had been a while since he had been with a woman.

The last time had been the night with the white chick. It had been Sunil and Shivraj's idea, he had just gone along with it, and Anil was always so drunk and stoned, he never knew what he was doing half the time. Mind you they had all been pretty wasted. A full evening of drinking and a few lines of coke in the toilets. The woman had pretended to struggle, but by the time Sunil and Shivraj had finished with her, she was compliant and didn't put up a fight when he had his turn. It was a pity they had to kill her, he would have liked another go, but as Sunil had reasoned, dead people can't tell tales.

Manish took another drink from the bottle. Maybe he would have Sujata. She wouldn't say anything. If she did, he would just send her back to the village. Plenty more where she came from. Manish stood up. He was hungry, still had a slight hangover from the night before, and now, he was feeling horny. He wanted nothing more than some solid food, but he had to lose a lot more weight. Sunil and Shivraj kept giving him a hard time about his weight, and after what happened to Anil, he realized he should take better care of himself. He finished the contents of the bottle, now used to the taste, and walked toward the changing room, all thoughts of finishing the workout replaced by the arousal his memories had stirred up. He would go home and see what the servant was doing.

The Land Cruiser was already waiting outside, two wheels up on the sidewalk but still creating enough obstruction for the traffic to slow and weave around it, his driver ignoring the honking and shouting from the other drivers. Manish opened the back door, threw his bag on the back seat, and climbed in.

"Home," he grunted at his driver and settled back in the seat. His stomach gurgled disturbingly. The draught beer they drank last night must have been a bit off. Tonight, he would suggest to Sunil and Shivraj they go somewhere else for a drink. The Land-Cruiser slowed at the gate, and the watchman jumped up from his plastic chair to push the gates open so it could pull inside. Manish climbed out, suddenly feeling a bit worse for wear. His chest felt tight, and he was really starting to feel sick. Walking inside, he saw Sujata crouched down, mopping the floor with a large cloth, but he had changed his mind. She could wait until he felt a bit better.

33

Sujata straightened up and stretched her back out. This house was so big, mopping the floors was playing havoc with her back. Why did people have to live in such big houses? There were only three people living there. Back home, the whole village could live in a house this size. She wiped the sweat from her forehead and adjusted her sari. She wasn't allowed to keep the air-conditioning on when her boss wasn't at home, and the house soon heated up. Sir was at his office, and Madam was no doubt out at another one of her lunches. Their no-good son had risen late and gone to the gym, so she was alone in the house with just the cook for company. She was glad though. The way the fat idiot looked at her gave her the creeps. She knew what he wanted, she had seen it before from the old men in the village, so she was happy when he wasn't around. She finished mopping the marble floors in the living room and carried the bucket into the entrance hall.

It was hard work, but she needed the money. Ever since her father got sick, he couldn't work in the fields, and her income was the only money they had. The money her mother earned from selling vegetables wasn't enough to support them.

Sujata wrung the excess water from the mopping cloth and crouched down to wipe the floor as the front door opened. The fat boy walked in, and she kept her head down, avoiding eye contact, expecting a comment from him, but nothing came. He walked past without saying anything, and she stole a look from the corner of her eye. His skin was pale and his forehead slick with a sheen of sweat. He will have a heart attack one day, she thought and resumed wiping the floor. She heard him climb the stairs to the first floor, his breath labored, his pace slow. She turned to watch him.

Something wasn't right. As he neared the top of the stairs, he hesitated and dropped to one knee, his left hand grabbing the stair rail for support. Sujata gasped as his body swayed, then hit the wall with a thud. He gasped for air and clutched at his chest with both hands. His body slipped down a step, then Sujata screamed as he tipped over and tumbled backward down the stairs.

34

Inspector Rajiv Sampath put down his pen and rubbed his eyes. It had been a long night. At two a.m., he had been called from his home to inspect a suicide scene. A young newlywed girl had been found hanging from a ceiling fan. Rajiv suspected there was more to it than met the eye, her death possibly prompted by unreasonable dowry demands, and he knew a more thorough investigation would be needed. He could never understand why people couldn't just get along and live peacefully. By the time he had finished inspecting the scene and gone back to the station to file a report, it hadn't been worth going back home. He looked at his watch, it was just after seven in the morning. Time to give his long-suffering wife a call and let her know he wouldn't be home until the evening. He would try to finish early if the workload allowed him; he sorely needed sleep. There had been too many interrupted nights this week, and it was catching up with him. Rajiv yawned as he dialed the number.

"Someone, bring me some coffee," he called out.

A piping hot cup of South Indian filter coffee arrived

with the morning's papers. Rajiv heaped two spoons of sugar into his coffee—he could do that here in the station. His wife never allowed it at home, ever mindful of his health. Sitting back he took a sip, the hot sweet liquid giving him an instant lift. He licked his lips, set the cup down and turned to the papers. The headlines were filled with the usual nonsense. Political bickering interspersed with film and cricket gossip. He flicked through the pages, not bothering to read in depth, preferring to get an overview of what was going on in the incredibly complicated country he lived in.

In the local news, there was already a report on the girl's suicide the previous night. He shook his head. It was unbelievable how fast the news gets out. He scanned his eyes over the article, the reporter already talking up the details, hinting at harassment from the in-laws. The reporter was probably right but should at least give Rajiv time for an investigation. Rajiv was about to turn the page when another article caught his eye.

"Manish Nayak, only son of industrialist Sriram Nayak, died of a heart attack on Wednesday after returning from the gym." Manish Nayak. Manish Nayak. The name was familiar. Rajiv closed his eyes, clearing his mind, letting his subconscious do the work. Ah yes, he remembered the guy. An overweight rich kid who hung about in bars all the time. He and his friends were always involved in trouble, but nothing could ever be pinned on them, such was the influence of their fathers.

Rajiv had little sympathy for these spoilt sons of powerful men. Rajiv had come up the hard way. His parents had saved hard for him to enter the police academy, his mother selling all her wedding jewelry, and both parents sacrificing their lifestyle for years to ensure his education.

These rich kids never had to try hard for anything in their lives, everything handed to them on a platter.

Rajiv folded the papers and pushed them to one side and grabbed the next folder on the pile of files heaped on the desk. He certainly hadn't anticipated this much paperwork when he joined the police. He sighed and opened the file. In the deepest recesses of his mind though there was something gnawing away at his memory. Something about Manish Nayak's death but he couldn't make the connection. He knew it would come to him in time, it always did, and started reading the file.

35

Three days had passed since John had visited the gym. Three days in which he had stayed home, not wanting to go anywhere near Sunil's house. He felt strangely at peace but couldn't understand why. His conscious mind told him he was responsible for the deaths of two people that he should be feeling guilty. But he didn't. When he thought of what he had done, all he could picture was Charlotte's smiling face as if somewhere beyond the grave she knew what he was doing for her, and she approved. He spent the days packing up the house and finally, allowed himself to finish clearing out the studio. The paints and unbroken brushes he kept to one side to be donated to an orphanage or a school with the spare canvases and the easel. The paintings he would send back to Winchester, to Charlotte's parents. Except for Charlotte's last painting, the almost finished landscape of the Western Ghats. That was his, he wouldn't give it to anyone. He carried it downstairs and leaned the canvas against the wall in the living room where he could look at it from his armchair.

On the morning of the fourth day, John heard a knock on the door and looked out the window to see a police Bolero parked out front. His heart skipped a beat, and he stepped back quickly from the window. What should he do? He could pretend he wasn't home, but his car was parked in the carport. Fuck. Another knock on the door. He took a deep breath. No, he had to face them. Anyway, there was nothing to link him to the two deaths as far as he was aware. He had to act and behave normally as if nothing had happened. He took another deep breath and exhaled slowly, attempting to breathe out the tension. It didn't work. Walking to the door, he opened it just as it was knocked for the third time.

"Mr. Hayes."

"Inspector." John looked around. Apart from Inspector Rajiv, there was no one else around, not even his driver today.

"Can I come in?"

"Sorry, yes, of course." John stepped to one side and allowed Rajiv to enter. He walked through into the living room and waited expectantly.

"Please, sit down." John waved to the armchair. "What brings you here?"

"I was just passing by and thought I would come and see you. How are you keeping up? Have you finished your packing?"

"Almost," John smiled, not sure where the conversation was going. Was he really just here as a courtesy visit? "It has taken me longer than I thought, and I have had a few things to sort out with work."

Rajiv nodded sympathetically. "Yes, I thought you were planning to have left by now."

"Well, you know how it is here. Things don't always go to schedule."

"Indeed," Rajiv nodded. "That's a nice painting."

"The last one Charlotte painted."

"Oh, ah, it's very nice."

They sat in an uncomfortable silence for a while, both of them staring at the painting, Rajiv unsure of what to say next, and John lost in his memories. Eventually, John broke the silence.

"Can I get you some tea or coffee?"

"No, no, I had better be going. Thank you." Rajiv stood and moved toward the door. John stood too, and as he did so, Rajiv turned as if an afterthought. "Do you remember the news clipping you showed me a couple of weeks ago, the one of the man you believed was involved in the... ah, unfortunate incident with Mrs. Hayes."

John's heart beat faster. "Yes, I do, why?"

"Do you have it with you?"

John's mind raced. What does he mean? What does he want? He swallowed nervously. "I'm not sure. I think I threw it away when you didn't believe me. Why do you ask?"

"It's okay," Rajiv nodded and looked at John thoughtfully. "It's just an unusual thing has happened." He opened the front door as John waited expectantly. He turned back to look at John again.

"Two of the friends of the man whose picture you showed me have died in the last two weeks." He paused and studied John's face.

John willed himself to meet Rajiv's gaze without flinching. "Really? That's good if they were involved. They don't deserve to live after what they did."

"Well, if it was them, perhaps you are right, Mr. Hayes. It

just seems a strange coincidence. And in my job, there are not many coincidences."

"How did they die?"

"One was run over by a car as he slept in the road. Apparently, he was drunk."

John nodded, careful to not let his expression give anything away. "They say drinking and driving don't mix."

"Ha, yes, Mr. Hayes. Very funny."

"And the other?"

"He had a heart attack at home after returning from the gym."

"Sounds like an unfortunate couple of events. Perhaps it's karma? You believe in karma, don't you, Detective?"

Rajiv narrowed his eyes, then nodded. He turned to leave, stepping outside and down the two steps from the front door, then turned back.

"I believe in karma, Mr. Hayes, but I also believe in the rule of law. That's the only thing from keeping us from being savages."

John stepped outside feeling more confident as Rajiv was leaving. "Your rule of law didn't prevent the savages from mutilating my wife."

Rajiv climbed into his Bolero and looked down at the steering column, a sad expression filling his face. "No Mr. Hayes, and I am truly sorry about that." He started the engine and looked up. "You are a good man, Mr. Hayes. I like you. Don't go and do anything you might regret."

36

S unil stood dressed all in white in a cotton *Kurta* and pajama, his hands clasped in front of him and looked down at the floor avoiding eye contact. Manish's mother sobbed quietly in the corner, surrounded by somber looking women. The room was filled with people, also dressed in white, and yet more were filing in and out of the door. Sunil hated funerals. They depressed him, and he had only come to this one out of respect for Manish. The poor, fat fucker. How many times had they told him to lose weight, to exercise? The crazy thing was Manish had joined the gym, and they hadn't known. But it looked like that was what had killed him, over-exertion leading to a heart attack.

Sunil looked around the room at the people who had come to pay their respects. Most weren't even friends of Manish but friends of the parents or people attempting to win favor with Manish's father. Everyone seemed to hang around rich people, thinking it would rub off on them. Sunil wondered how many people would come to his funeral and whether they would only come because of his dad's position. Despite the occasion, he smiled. He wasn't going to die just yet. He caught Shivraj's eye across the room. At least Shivraj didn't have to dress especially for the occasion, he always wore white. With a flick of his eyes and a jerk of his head, he indicated to meet him outside and made his way to the door, nodding and shaking the hands of those people he knew. Once outside, he waited in the front garden, reaching into his pocket for his cigarettes and lighting one. He took a deep puff and blew the smoke into the air as Shivraj walked out the door and joined him. They nodded to each other and stood in silence for a while, Sunil smoking, Shivraj digging a hole with his heel in the beautifully manicured lawn. Sunil flicked his cigarette butt into the undergrowth.

"Silly bugger. We told him to lose some weight. Looks like he went and overdid it."

Shivraj nodded but didn't say anything, contemplating the hole he had made.

"Fuck, I need a drink, let's get out of here."

Shivraj looked up and regarded Sunil for a moment. "Don't you think it's strange that both Anil and Manish have died in the last two weeks?"

"Yeah, it is strange. It's fucking sad too."

"Yeah, but it's weird, right?"

Sunil's eyes narrowed, and he glared at Shivraj. "What are you trying to say?"

"No, it's just..." Shivraj hesitated.

"What?"

"Well, what if one of us is next?"

"Fuck off. Why would one of us be next?" Sunil blurted hurriedly, quelling the disturbing thought which was rising from the back of his mind.

"Maybe it's karma? Maybe it's..." Shivraj lowered his voice, "Because of what we did with that white woman?"

"Quiet!" hissed Sunil, looking around to make sure they hadn't been overheard. "I told you never to mention that again. Anyway, you weren't complaining at the time. In fact, from the look on your face, you enjoyed it."

"Yeah, but..." he trailed off.

"But nothing. You spend too much time praying and believing in all this superstitious crap. It's all bullshit people like us make up to keep these bloody villagers in line. I can't believe you are thinking the same way."

"Yeah maybe you are right," Shivraj didn't sound convinced. "Come on, let's get out of here and grab a drink."

Sunil scowled at Shivraj's back as he walked toward the front gate. He didn't like to believe in this crap, he left that for his mother and the stupid priests who were always leeching off her. But like it or not, the seed of doubt was starting to grow in his mind. Fuck it! Time for a drink. He followed Shivraj out onto the street.

37

The warm rays of the morning sun fell on John's face as he sat in the garden chair, a steaming mug of coffee in his hand, a half-empty French press on the table beside him. Two squirrels carried on an animated conversation with each other on the boundary wall, bobbing their heads, flicking their tails back and forth, and squeaking repetitively. John took a sip of his coffee and allowed his mind to run back over the events of the past few days. The visit from Rajiv had shaken him up, but following that, nothing had happened. There had been no talk of foul play in the press, the news instead filled with the usual bickering between political parties and talk of the latest Bollywood romance. John had disposed of the remains of the *Cerbera* seeds, scattering them on the roadside in farmland to the north of the city, burnt the gloves and discarded Manish's water bottle in a dumpster in one of the suburbs to the south of Bangalore. No doubt by now, it had been found by a rag picker and was being re-purposed. In this city of eight million people, it would never be traced back to him or to Manish's death.

He topped up his coffee mug from the French press and leaned back in his chair. By rights, he should be feeling guilty, but he felt nothing of the sort. Instead, he felt strangely at peace, a calmness he hadn't felt for months. He still thought of Charlotte every day, missed her with every particle of his being, but somehow, in some way, the action he was taking was giving him some peace of mind, some sort of closure.

Charlotte had been a peace-loving woman, but one thing she never could stand was injustice, and she often stood up to defend herself and others when she felt a wrong was committed. John knew she would have approved of his actions. These guys needed to be punished. The system was broken and wouldn't do it. If he didn't stop them, who was to say they wouldn't do it again? And who knew how many times they had done it before? No, he was on the right path —halfway done and he wouldn't stop until all of them were burning in hell.

He had got rid of the easy targets. Swami and Sunil were bound to be more difficult. He also had to make sure nothing linked back to him. With each death, suspicion would rise as had been proven by Inspector Rajiv's visit to his house. He would have to be extra careful from now on.

38

S unil sat on the roof terrace, a cigarette in his hand, a pile of butts overflowing the ashtray onto the table. He had risen uncharacteristically early, having slept badly, the bottle of Black Label he had consumed with Shivraj the night before not helping him sleep, and now, he was tired and had a splitting headache. He lit another cigarette from the butt of his old one and took a long drag, holding the smoke in before expelling it in a cloud above his head, the nicotine helping to smooth the edges off his hangover. He had told Shivraj he was talking nonsense, it was purely coincidence Manish and Anil had died, but deep down, he had a gnawing doubt. He wasn't superstitious, all that karma and God stuff was all bullshit, invented to keep the masses in their place.

No, he was the son of Surya Patil, and he was in control of his own destiny. He was a man of action—if he wanted something, he would get it, if he wanted something to happen in a certain way, he would make sure it happened in that way. Manish, Anil, and Shivraj—they were all weak. Shivraj, who rode around in his jeep dressed in white, pretending he was a great student leader was only in the position because Sunil's father was the leader of the Party. If he hadn't been Sunil's friend, he would be nothing.

Sunil thought back to what Shivraj had mentioned yesterday—that night with the white whore. That stupid driver who had hit his car, he had deserved everything he got, the dirty villager. Sunil had enjoyed giving him a good kicking. Beating the shit out of someone always made him aroused, the feeling of power over another, and when he heard the white bitch screaming from the back of the car, he couldn't help himself—her beautiful white skin, her perfectly formed breasts, smaller than he liked, but at least she wasn't fat like some of the other women he'd had. No, she looked like she worked out. He felt a stirring in his groin as he remembered. It had been his idea to take her. No-one was around, no one would know. He would have his bit of foreign pussy. The others had joined in happily, filled with excitement and bloodlust after kicking the shit out of that feeble driver. But after they had all taken their turn, their lust spent, the adrenaline gone, they had become weak and scared. He had taken control. He had strangled the bitch, made sure no one could ever tell the story of that night— just like he had done before—tying up loose ends. That was what made him stand apart. That's what had made him survive this long without getting caught. He was the one in charge, he made his own karma, he decided his own destiny, not some fucking made up gods. Flicking his cigarette butt onto the floor, he stood and walked to the edge of the roof terrace and looked down at the front gate.

"Manju," he shouted.

The elderly watchman jumped up from his plastic chair and looked up. "Sir?"

"Come here."

39

Manjunath had worked for the Patil family for twenty years. Patil Sir treated him well, had given him money when his wife was sick, and when his neighbors in the village had wanted to take his piece of farmland off him, Patil Sir had sent his party workers to sort them out. It was good working for such a powerful man. Proximity to power had its benefits. Now as Manjunath rushed inside the gate, he thought of the son. Patil Sir had come up the hard way, had built himself into one of the most powerful leaders in the state through hard work and clever political wrangling. His son, however, spent his days drinking and smoking and ordering the staff around. He wasn't a good man like his father, and Manjunath didn't like him. The son had never done a day's work in his life.

Manjunath slipped off his sandals and entered the house barefoot, climbing the stairs to the roof terrace. He didn't like the arrogant young man at all, but he couldn't show it. He had seen what the son could do when he was angry, and he wanted to avoid being on the receiving end.

Manjunath reached the top level of the house and rushed out onto the terrace. He folded his hands in front of him and bowed his head, looking meekly at the ground.

"Sir?"

"What took you so long?"

"Sir?" Manjunath looked up, then quickly looked down again. The spoilt brat was obviously not in a good mood.

"That cop you always talk to. The one who patrols this area. What's his name?"

"Constable Ravi, Sir."

"Tell him to come and see me."

"Yes, Sir." Manjunath couldn't understand what Sunil wanted with Ravi, but he wasn't about to question him.

"Go!"

"Yes, Sir," Manjunath turned and rushed off the terrace, glad he had got away lightly.

40

Constable Ravindra Srivastava liked to think of himself as a practical man. It had been fifteen years since he joined the force, enrolling from his village on the West Coast of Karnataka. His career in the police hadn't turned out to be what he had dreamed of when he signed up, but he had adapted. He couldn't change the system, so he didn't bother. Instead, he looked at ways in which he could supplement his meager police salary, and if that meant stealing files from the station for Sunil Patil, that's what he would do. The money would help him buy a plot of land in the village. Land on which he would build a little house for himself and his wife to retire to. He would even keep a bit of money aside for his wife. She hadn't bought a new sari in a long while, it was about time she got something nice for herself.

He stood in the file room, a dusty space at the rear of the station and looked around at the rows of battered steel cabinets stuffed to overflowing with files. He wasn't worried about being caught. It was normal for a constable to visit the room to pull out files. It happened every day. The difference was Ravi had no intention of returning what he took. Ravi compared the number he had written in pen on the palm of his hand with those written on the cabinets until he found the one that matched. Pulling open the top drawer, he searched through the files, but it wasn't there, so he pulled out the middle drawer. Three files back was the one he wanted. He pushed the filing cabinet drawer shut and slipped the file into a large brown paper envelope which he tucked under his arm as he walked out. He doubted anyone would notice it was missing, and they wouldn't connect it with him if they did. So many people had access to the room, and no one even looked in his direction as he walked out the front door of the station and over to the motorcycle parking.

Opening up the saddlebag strapped to the side of his Royal Enfield Bullet, he slipped the envelope in before throwing his leg over the bike. He raised the stand and twisted the key in the ignition, coaxing the 500cc single-cylinder engine into life. It rattled reluctantly before settling into its characteristic thumping idle. The bike was his pride and joy. He had dreamed of getting one since he was a boy but would have struggled to afford one on his police salary alone. It was only the extra cash for doing jobs for people like Sunil Patil that enabled him to realize his childhood dream. He took the helmet from where it was hanging on the handlebars and pulled it on over his head, leaving the chin strap hanging. Twisting the throttle, he gave the engine a rev and rumbled out of the station car park, disappearing into the honking steam of traffic.

41

The jeep pulled up outside the Meenakshi Temple on the edge of Shivnagar.

Shivraj Gowda, the young man John knew as Swami, jumped out and directed the three young men with him to unload the sacks of rice and bundles of flowers from the rear before following him into the temple. Once inside Shivraj looked around, spotting the head priest at the rear of the temple deep in conversation with a young couple. He caught his eye, and the priest realizing who it was, made his excuses and rushed over, raising his hands in prayer.

"Welcome, welcome. *Devi Ashirvada*. Blessings of the Goddess."

"*Devi Ashirvada*," Shivraj replied, his hands held in prayer.

"Always good to see you, Sir." Despite the priest being old enough to be Shivraj's father, he still deferred to him, knowing full well his political connections. Even God's workers knew where the real power lay.

Shivraj smiled, "*Panditji,* I have come to make some offerings. I want you to do a *Pooja* for me as soon as possible.

I will, of course, also make a generous cash donation to the temple."

"Of course, of course, Sir." News of the cash donation spurred the elderly priest into rapid action. He waved at another younger priest and indicated to Shivraj's men to follow him with the offerings. "For what purpose is the *Pooja*? Is it for wealth, or..." the priest leaned in closer and lowered his voice, "have you decided it's time to take a wife?" He straightened up and winked at Shivraj.

Shivraj did little to hide his irritation with the priest's comment. "No," he snapped. He took a breath, composed himself and then replied, "Let's just say I want to remove some bad luck."

The priest nodded thoughtfully, "Yes we can do a *Pooja* for you. But I can give you a powerful mantra as well. Just repeat it throughout the day. It will help a lot. Of course, we will need to do the *Pooja* as well," he added, hoping he hadn't just talked himself out of the cash donation. He needn't have worried.

"I have important work. I don't have time to be saying mantras all day. That's what I am paying you for."

"Yes, of course, I will start right away. Is there anything else I can do for you?"

Shivraj shook his head. "No, that will be all. But make sure it's done as soon as possible."

The priest nodded effusively, "Of course, of course. Ah, Sir how much will the donation be?"

Shivraj fixed him with a hard stare. "It will be generous." He beckoned to one of his men and whispered in his ear. The young man went outside to the jeep and returned with a sports bag, passing it over to Shivraj. Shivraj unzipped it half way and showed the contents to the priest whose eyes widened and he bobbed his head from side to side.

"Very generous of you, Sir. Very generous. The Mother's blessings will be showered upon you."

Shivraj nodded. "Good. Remember, as soon as possible." These priests were all the same. Still, it didn't hurt to request divine intervention to remove the bad luck heading his way which had already claimed the lives of Anil and Manish.

He turned away from the priest and started to walk out of the temple. Just before the door, he hesitated and turned around. Looking at the idol, he pressed his hands together in front of his chest, closed his eyes, and said a silent prayer. He then turned and marched out of the temple, his men following closely behind him. That's the divine side of things looked after. Now to deal with the matter Sunil had raised.

42

John watched from the front seat of his SUV parked over a hundred meters away in the shade of a large Jacaranda. He knew Shivraj visited the temple once a week, but usually on a Thursday and normally, alone. Today was not a Thursday. It was the first time John had seen Shivraj go with his men and numerous bags.

John waited until Shivraj's jeep had pulled away before getting out of the car and walking toward the temple. He slipped off his shoes at the entrance, keeping them in the shoe rack provided and walked inside, ignoring the curious stares from the other worshippers. He paused to let his eyes adjust to the dim light inside, then rang the bell suspended above the entrance to inform the deity of his arrival as was the custom. Walking further inside, he approached the sanctum sanctorum. On a sparkling golden throne sat a life-size statue of a beautiful goddess wrapped in a red and gold sari with garlands of fresh marigolds around her neck. At her feet were bowls of fruit and sweets while on each side stood two brass oil lamps, their wicks lit, the flames flickering back and forth. Tendrils of sandalwood smoke from incense sticks wafted in front of her and climbed lazily to the ceiling. John stood and let the atmosphere soak through him.

Indian temples were often noisy and full of activity, but whenever he had entered one, despite the hustle and bustle, he felt an inner peace. He wasn't a religious man, by any means, but he did believe in some form of higher power, whatever you chose to call it, and he felt it then. He folded his hands in prayer and knelt before the goddess. He closed his eyes and prayed.

"Dear God, please forgive me for any wrongs I may be doing, but please give me the strength and conviction to continue. I ask you please to watch over Charlotte wherever she is, to bless her and look after her. And I ask you, please, dear God, to help me bring down my vengeance on those who harmed her." He opened his eyes and looked around self-consciously, aware he was conspicuous as the only non-Indian in the temple. But apart from the initial curiosity, everyone ignored him and went about their own business.

Turning his attention toward the priests, he watched them prepare for a ceremony. They piled in one corner the bags of rice Shivraj's men had carried in while another priest carried the bundles of flowers toward the idol where he unwrapped them and placed them at the feet of the Goddess. An older priest stood to the side, a sports bag in his hand, a contented look on his face, watching the activities before turning and entering a side door, taking the bag with him.

John smiled to himself. Perhaps Shivraj was feeling rattled.

S unil and Shivraj sat in Shivraj's jeep on the edge of the slum, Sunil chain smoking while Shivraj sat nervously tapping his fingers on the steering wheel. Sunil scanned the faces of every man who walked past, each time comparing them with a photo in his lap. They had been there for an hour, and Sunil was getting irritated.

"Fucking stinks around here," he grumbled. "Why don't you get a decent vehicle, something with air con?"

Shivraj shook his head. "I like my jeep."

"Come on man. Take some money from the party funds, get yourself a decent car. At least I wouldn't have to sit here sweating away, breathing in this stench from the fucking slums. Lazy fuckers. Look at them. Won't do a decent day's work, all of them expecting a handout from the government. From my father!" He gestured toward a man sitting on the curb, his head slumped on his chest, eyes closed as he swayed from side to side in a drunken stupor, a dark stain on his pants where he had pissed himself. "Look at him, he should be fucking working. He's blind drunk." Sunil glanced at his gold Rolex. "It's ten am, and he's fucking drunk already."

Shivraj ignored his grumbling, his fingers continuing their uneasy beat.

Sunil stiffened as a thin man in suit pants, a loose work shirt, sandals, his hair slicked back with coconut oil walked out of the slum and onto the main road where they were parked. Sunil narrowed his eyes to get a good look, comparing him with the photo in his hand.

"That's him."

"Are you sure?"

"Of course, I'm fucking sure, get a move on!"

Sunil flicked his unfinished cigarette onto the road as

Shivraj started up the jeep. He pulled away from the curb and mashed his foot on the accelerator, heading directly toward the man. He skidded to a stop in front of him, blocking his way, and Sunil jumped out, grabbing the man by the shirt, and punched him in the stomach. He doubled over gasping for air, and Sunil followed up with a knee to his face splitting his lip and breaking a few teeth. The man dropped to his knees, blood running from his mouth, and held his hands up, pleading for Sunil to leave him alone, but Sunil ignored him, stepping closer and punching him in the face, knocking him flat on the ground. A woman screamed while others stopped and stared, too scared to do anything but watch. The traffic bunched up around them as cars slowed to take a look before moving on. Sunil ignored them, confident no one would say anything while Shivraj watched uneasily from the driver's seat. Sunil grabbed hold of the man's shirt and hauled him up off the ground, throwing him into the back of the jeep where he lay curled up and whimpering, his face bloodied and bruised. Sunil jumped into the front seat as Shivraj revved the engine and stomped on the gas, spinning the wheels in the dirt, disappearing up the road in a cloud of dust. The passers-by watched the jeep leave, before once again carrying on their daily business. Of course, no one would remember seeing anything.

43

Inspector Rajiv Sampath crouched down beside the body, pulled back the sheet and looked down at the battered and badly bruised face. The eyes were swollen into slits, the nose twisted to one side, and dried blood caked both sides of the face. Several teeth were missing from the open mouth, and the lips were split in several places. He pulled the sheet back even further and looked down at the naked torso, the skin mottled black, purple, and yellow. There was barely an untouched portion of flesh on the body. Rajiv looked again at the head. He wouldn't need the Medical Examiner's report, the cause of death clear, the neck obviously broken. With a deep sigh, Rajiv recovered the body with the sheet. Seven months ago, he had seen the same face, battered even then, but alive, its owner sitting up in a hospital bed. This was definitely not a coincidence. Rajiv had taken this man's statement, and because of that, the man was now dead, his body mutilated and dumped in a ditch.

He rose, straightened his uniform tunic, took a deep breath, and exhaled completely, trying unsuccessfully to quell the anger building inside him. He signaled to one of the uniformed constables to take the body away and watched as they loaded the body into the back of an ambulance. Rajiv's gut told him who was responsible, but he knew deep down there was nothing he could do about it. The question was how had they found out about Sanjay? His identity had never been made public, confined only to the police records. That meant one of his own men had betrayed him. Rajiv shook his head in frustration and kicked the tire of his Bolero.

His driver looked at him in surprise, "Sir? Is something wrong?"

"Everything is wrong." He climbed into the driver's seat. "Get in, I'm driving."

Rajiv twisted the key in the ignition and stamped his foot on the accelerator. The system was rotten to the core. He couldn't even trust his own men to uphold the very laws that prevented society from descending into barbarity.

44

John took the news calmly at first, and it surprised him. It was as if he had become numb, had lost the ability to feel emotion. Was this what happened to soldiers in wartime? Perhaps it was nature's way of protecting them from devastating feelings of loss so the body and mind could continue to function. It seemed to be working that way for him. John felt as if he was outside himself, observing from afar the events happening to the person called John Hayes as if watching a character in a movie.

Rajiv sat opposite, nursing a glass of whiskey, his second. He had said little since he arrived and delivered the bad news, obviously deeply troubled, and it was clear something was on his mind. John was content to give him space and time to express himself in his own way and watched him as he swirled the amber fluid around the glass, staring morosely at the floor.

They sat in silence for a while before Rajiv looked up at John, the twitches in his face and the flickering of his eyes hinting at a fierce internal dialogue.

"I'm a good man, Mr. Hayes. I work hard, I obey the laws, and I do all I can to make my little part of the world a better, safer place. A place where ordinary people can go about their lives without living in fear. That's why I joined the police force. To make a difference. To uphold the laws of our society." He looked down again and sighed.

John nodded slowly and took a sip of his gin.

"The system is broken, Mr. Hayes," Rajiv spoke into his glass. "Rotten. We live in a world where the powerful prey on the weak, the rich prey on the poor. The rule of the bully. You've heard this expression 'Might is right,' no?"

John nodded.

"It's been seventy years since we gained our independence from the tyranny of British rule—no offense to you, Mr. Hayes—but little has changed. We are supposed to be free. We live in the largest democracy in the world, Mr. Hayes. But to what benefit? It's the rich and powerful who continue to rule over us. The common man has no rights, no freedom. What was the point of gaining our independence? There are so many people like me Mr. Hayes, who want to make a difference, who want to make our country a country we can be proud of. But the system beats us down every time. Greed, corruption, selfishness. It's just too hard." He shook his head, exasperated.

John wasn't sure how to reply. He didn't think anything he could say would make Rajiv feel any better. He let his mind wander to the last time he had seen Sanjay, in his little home with his wife Pournima and their two young daughters. He thought of the life that now awaited those girls with no father, no income coming into the house. What future would they have? He remembered the kindness Pournima had shown him, the food she had sent for him, the hospitality she had offered.

Finally, he started to feel a little emotion. Not so much sadness, which surprised him. Did that make him a bad person? He had killed two people and now was unable to feel for others? He did feel sadness and loss, but only for Charlotte. Was he being selfish? He wasn't sure. He did feel guilty though, that was the predominant emotion. Would Sanjay be alive today if he hadn't killed Anil and Manish? Probably yes. Perhaps he should have left the country and returned to England. The girls would still have a father, Pournima would still have her husband.

As if sensing what John was thinking, Rajiv looked up and fixed his gaze on John. "The two men that died, Mr. Hayes. Anil Goswami and Manish Nayak."

John tensed, not sure where the conversation was heading.

"Whatever happened to those two men, Mr. Hayes, they deserved to die. I am sure, now that Sanjay has been killed, they were directly involved in what happened to your wife. There is no other explanation. He was a good man, a father. He wasn't involved in anything bad, he had no enemies. But he gave a witness statement, then he was killed. I haven't lasted this long as a Police Inspector by believing in coincidences, Mr. Hayes."

John interrupted, "Please, call me John."

Rajiv nodded, before continuing. "Am I right in assuming Sanjay gave you the newspaper clipping identifying Sunil Patil?"

John nodded and drained his drink before setting the glass down on the floor. He sat back in his chair, waiting for Rajiv to continue.

"I thought so." Rajiv paused, thinking of how best to resolve the conflicted thoughts in his mind. He stood up and paced around the room. Turning to John, he said, "The way

I see it Mr., ah John, let's agree Sanjay was right. Two of the men are dead... apparently of natural causes." He paused, looking at John for a reaction. John looked back expressionless, maintaining eye contact. Rajiv turned and walked across the room again, talking as he paced.

"The two men died, and suddenly, Sanjay is killed. Someone got spooked, and my money is on the remaining two friends. It's a tragedy what has happened to Sanjay. Terrible." He paused, shaking his head, and looked down at the floor. "But it shows how these people think they can get away with anything. If those men hadn't died, they would have lived the rest of their life doing whatever they like, knowing they can get away with it. Who knows how many other women it could happen to, how many other lives they will destroy while living in their big houses, driving their fancy cars? They deserved to be punished, and the system can't do it. In a way John, I am happy that..." he looked closely at John, "their karma caught up with them."

John regarded him carefully, not sure what to say. Instead, he picked up his glass, realized it was empty and put it down again.

Rajiv went back to his seat, sat down, and examined his glass as if embarrassed by his outburst. After a few minutes of silence, he drained his glass and set it down on the floor beside his chair before standing again. He looked down at John.

"If karma were to catch up with the other two, let's just say I won't be looking too closely. Good night, John." He turned and let himself out.

John sat and listened to the sound of Rajiv's vehicle leaving, not moving, staring at the floor. Absentmindedly, he picked up his glass, empty but for the half-melted remains of an ice cube and swirled it around. He tipped the ice-cold water into his mouth and crunched on the pieces of ice while setting the glass down. Rightly or wrongly, he had set out on a path, and he would finish what he had begun. He owed it to Charlotte, and now, he owed it to Sanjay. His death would not be in vain. Despite the gravity of the situation, he grinned to himself. He also, in a way, owed it to Inspector Rajiv Sampath.

45

S hivraj Gowda was going to be difficult. He was hardly ever alone. His days were filled with work for the Progressive People's Alliance Party, and he was constantly surrounded by party workers and supplicants. When he wasn't working, he spent most of his time with Sunil, only going home to sleep late at night. Anil had been an accident, and Manish had been relatively easy. Shivraj would require considerable thought and planning, and despite what Rajiv had said about looking the other way, John had to make sure nothing linked back to him. Sunil and Shivraj were now on edge. Their murder of Sanjay had shown they were rattled, and from what John had observed, it seemed to be affecting Shivraj more. After instructing the priests at the Meenakshi temple to perform a *Pooja* for him, Shivraj had visited the temple almost every second day since then, and he was looking noticeably tense. As John watched him from a distance, he seemed less cocky, his body language more nervous. He was constantly looking around, eyes scanning the street, and John had to be extra careful to ensure he wasn't spotted.

John thought about poisoning him with the same *Cerbera* seeds he had used on Manish, but he had disposed of the powdered seeds as soon as Manish had died, in fear of being caught, and he didn't want to risk using the same method again, in case the police re-examined Manish's death. Plus, he would have to drive all the way back to Kerala to get more.

He could run him over like he had done with Anil but soon dismissed the idea. With Anil, it had been a chance event, and John wasn't about to risk damaging his car—that could be used as evidence against him. He could use another car but had no idea how to steal one. No, he had to think of something else, something different. John knew there was a way, he just hadn't found it yet. This time, however, he would have to get his hands dirty, no more killing from afar. He intended to hurt Sunil and Shivraj. Make them feel pain before ending their lives. He owed it to Sanjay.

46

In central Bangalore, close to M.G. Road lies the predominantly Muslim suburb of Shivajinagar. Nestled in the middle, surrounded by furniture shops and stainless-steel traders is Russell Market, a chaotic mess of vegetable, fruit, and meat vendors, fighting to make themselves heard above the honking of traffic. Built over a hundred years ago by the British, the market still supplied many of the restaurants and hotels in the city.

It took John over an hour to travel the thirteen kilometers from his home to the market, the morning rush hour extending to mid-day as the city struggled to keep up with its rapidly expanding population. By the time he drove past the St Mary's Basilica and turned left into M.F. Norrona Street, he was exhausted and not in the best of moods.

Crowds of people spilled off the footpaths onto the roads, and he had to drive slowly and carefully. Scooters headed toward him on the wrong side of the street, and he swerved to avoid a small herd of cows occupying the middle of the road, chewing their cud as if they were alone in a field.

Parking was always a nightmare, but today he got lucky. One of the unofficial parking attendants caught his eye and waved him forward to a just vacated space. John pulled forward, then selected reverse to move back into the vacant parking space. He ignored the barrage of horns and shouts from the vehicles and two-wheelers behind him and gently edged backward, leaving them to find their own way around him, in the way only Indian traffic can, like shoals of fish negotiating a reef.

He handed over twenty rupees to the attendant and bent down to roll up the legs of his jeans, the ground underfoot awash with rotting vegetables and dirty water. The market itself overflowed from the official building, and the footpath was partially blocked by the vegetable vendors who had no place inside, their wares spread out on plastic sheets. John had to force his way through the crowds, finding a gap wherever he could. The noise was deafening as people haggled over fruit and vegetables, and delivery boys on bicycles and scooters rang their bells and honked in an effort to get through. The area fascinated John, so different from shopping in a supermarket back in England. There were fruits and vegetables he had never seen before, let alone tasted, piled high in colorful pyramids or packed tightly in boxes of straw. Many vendors specialized in just one item, one lady selling only limes, the green and yellow fruit piled high in front of her. Another vendor dealt solely in onions, and he sat peeling the loose skin from each one, discarding it in the street where an opportunistic goat gobbled it up.

The chef of one of John's favorite restaurants was buying fish from a stall in front, and John ducked his head down and turned away. He couldn't afford to be spotted by anyone he knew. He turned down one of the side alleys, past a row of vendors selling greens—spinach, coriander, mustard leaves, dill—and headed toward the back. In the rear corner of the market were the chicken vendors, cages stacked high in front of their shops. Many of the cages were empty by mid-morning, but a few were still filled with live chickens, all of them white, crammed into the cages so they could barely move. It was not a pleasant sight—the smell and noise of hundreds of distressed chickens overpowering and reminded John why he preferred to buy a frozen chicken from the supermarket. He picked a vendor at random and scanned his eyes over the cages. He couldn't see what he was looking for, so he moved on to the one next door. He wanted a rooster. He could never understand why people bought roosters to eat, surely the meat was too tough, but John needed it for another purpose.

John negotiated with the vendor for a live rooster, haggling just a little, not wanting to attract too much attention by paying too much or by bargaining too hard. Once they agreed on a price, the vendor asked if he wanted it slaughtered, pointing inside the stall. A young man with a huge blood-stained meat cleaver in his hand smiled back at him. John shook his head, and the vendor trussed up the rooster's feet, holding the squawking bird upside down, its wings flapping and then placed it inside the hessian sack John had brought with him. Once inside, it quietened down, and John walked back to his parked Scorpio, stowing the bag in the passenger footwell.

Time for the next phase of his plan.

47

John parked in the carport and unlocked the front door, looking around to make sure he wasn't observed, but there was no one around in the middle of the day, the children at school and most of the parents at work or out shopping. Removing the bag from the car, he carried it inside, placing it on the kitchen floor. He turned on the Bluetooth speaker on the countertop and linked it to his phone before scrolling through to his playlist and hitting play, increasing the volume of the music to drown out any noise. From the cleaning cupboard, he removed a broom and laid the handle on the floor. Taking a deep breath, he bent down and opened up the sack. With his left hand, he grabbed the rooster's feet and lifted it out. "I'm sorry little fella." The bird, sensing what was about to happen, flapped its wings violently, squawking in panic, the music not quite loud enough to drown out the sound. John laid the bird on the floor and placed the broom handle over its neck, just behind the head. The rooster calmed down and laid there quietly, its wings spread out to either side. John paused for a moment gaining the courage for what he had to do next. He had Googled how to do it, but that didn't make it any easier.

He swallowed and with gritted teeth, grabbed hold of the rooster's feet with his left hand while at the same time standing on the broom handle with his right foot. He pulled the feet upwards sharply. He didn't hear a crack. Instead, the rooster squawked loudly and flapped its wings. He pulled again, the neck stretching noticeably. He let go of the feet and stepped back, the bird's nervous system taking over, flapping its wings and twitching before finally lying still. With remorse, John picked up the silent bird and laid its body on the kitchen counter-top. If people had to slaughter their own meat, the whole world would be vegetarian.

He took a kitchen knife and a plastic Ziploc bag and slit the throat of the rooster, holding the Ziploc bag underneath and allowing the blood to drain into the bag. Once it was full, he sealed it shut and left the remainder of the blood to drain out into the kitchen sink.

John realized he actually felt more remorse killing this bird than he did getting rid of Anil and Manish. But it had to be done. Now on to Phase Two.

ohn stiffened as a movement in his peripheral vision caught his attention but relaxed when he saw it was a stray dog stretching and yawning in the yellow glow of the street lamps. He pulled the dark navy baseball cap low on his head although being seen didn't seem to be much of a risk. John had picked the time carefully, reading somewhere three a.m. was the time when humans' circadian rhythms were at their lowest level of activity. It was one of the rare times of the day when the city was actually silent.

He refocused his attention on the modest house in front of him, built right to the boundary of its narrow site. A small entrance gate opened onto to a small concrete area, just room enough for keeping shoes and parking a scooter. At the rear of the space, two steps led up to the front door. The house was three stories high but was probably less than a quarter the size of Sunil's home. Shivraj, unlike his friends, didn't come from money, and despite his arrogance and cocky swagger, he too still lived with his parents. They weren't industrialists or politicians, but middle class, the father holding a nine-to-six office job in a local trading firm, his mother a stay-at-home mum.

Having satisfied himself no one was around, John made sure the car's interior light was in the off position and slowly opened the door. He took another look up and down the narrow street, pulling the baseball cap lower as he did so. Reaching across, he removed the hessian sack from the passenger seat and carefully pushed the door closed, allowing it to click shut with a minimum of noise. He walked briskly toward Shivraj's jeep where it was parked just one car along from his house. John kept close to the line of parked cars to reduce the chances of being spotted, and as he neared the jeep, he reached inside the sack and pulled out the carcass of the rooster. He laid it on the hood of the jeep, then removed the Ziploc bag, opened the top, and splashed the blood across the windscreen and hood. He put the Ziploc bag back inside the sack and walked swiftly back to his SUV. John grinned to himself. He couldn't wait to see Shivraj's reaction.

fter two hours of surprisingly peaceful sleep, John was back, parked at the end of the street, just close enough for him to see the front of the house and the jeep without being spotted. He reclined the seat slightly and settled down to wait.

By seven, the area was already active, several people up early to walk their dogs, others rushing out in office clothing and riding off to work on two-wheelers. John watched them all with one eye constantly on the house.

The front door opened, and he sat up as a middle-aged lady emerged in a paisley patterned nightdress, her long hair hanging loose and damp down her back as if it had just been washed. She walked the short distance to the front gate and picked up the plastic packet of milk left by the milk-man earlier that morning. She looked up the street, nodding at one of her neighbors returning from his morning walk and called out a greeting. As she turned to go back inside, her eyes caught sight of the front of the jeep. The packet of milk fell from her hand, and she screamed.

John grinned and wound down his window slightly so

he could hear what was happening. The neighbor rushed over to the lady who stood with her hand over her mouth, babbling what sounded like a prayer. From the house, an older man emerged, tufts of grey hair standing out from the side of his head, his thin legs wrapped in a *lungi*. He rushed over and held her by her shoulders, asking what was wrong. She pointed at the car, and his eyes widened. A small crowd gathered as neighbors appeared from the adjoining houses, everyone talking at once and gesticulating. Finally, Shivraj appeared in the doorway, rubbing the sleep from his face. He looked around at the crowd, then caught sight of his jeep. His mouth dropped open, and he took a step back.

John grinned. His plan was working.

The next night, John was back after spending the day online, researching black magic. He himself didn't believe in it, but from his research, he found there were still people in India who practiced black magic and many more who believed in it. Online there were hundreds of advertisements for people who could supposedly remove the effects of black magic, indicating the field of the dark art was ever present. John's view of it was more pragmatic. He believed the mere presence of a symbol associated with black magic would be enough to play on a superstitious person's mind, and their own thoughts would do the rest, sending them into a downward spiral. Having observed Shivraj for a while, John knew he liked to visit the temple once a week, prayed to the gods for support and blessings, and he was sure Shivraj would believe in black magic. Shivraj's reaction upon seeing the dead rooster and the blood had proven him right. In any event, even a non-believer would have to have a strong mind not to allow doubts to take hold in their head.

That day, John had bought a small rag doll and a small pot of black paint from a hobby shop. Taking them home, he had removed the clothing and hair from the doll, taking it back to its basic shape, and painted it black. The final touch was a large nail he had found in his toolkit which he used to pierce the doll's body in the heart.

50

S hivraj didn't feel good. He had slept badly, waking frequently drenched in sweat, his sleep haunted by the ghostly figure of a white woman. By six-thirty he gave up, splashed water on his face, and pulled on his ubiquitous white *Kurta* and pajama, not bothering to shower or shave. He thought back to the scene the previous morning. The blood, the dead chicken—all signs of Tantric practice. Someone was out to get him. Someone was applying black magic. But who? First Anil, then Manish, now it was his turn. His knees felt weak, and his stomach turned. He didn't want to die.

He walked downstairs where his mother was already awake, sitting in front of their home temple, rocking back and forth, lips moving in silent prayer. She hadn't eaten since the previous morning and had cried for most of the day. Shivraj had also lost his appetite and didn't bother to go to Sunil's in the evening for their customary drinks. Instead, he had gone to the temple with a big garland of flowers and a platter of fruit for the goddess. The head priest had given him a mantra for protection, and he had sat there for an hour, repeating it nonstop before leaving a big pile of cash in the donation box.

He would go again today for the morning *Aarti*, the offering of light to the goddess. He would take her blessings and seek her protection once more. She hadn't let him down so far. He crept past his mother and slowly opened the front door, sneaking out before she noticed. He slipped on his sandals and walked toward the jeep, reaching into his pocket for the keys. He was about to climb into the driver's seat when he looked down and saw a black doll with a nail through its heart, lying on the seat. His knees went weak, bile rose in his throat, and he turned and retched onto the road.

51

S unil found him later in the temple, kneeling in front of the idol, lips moving in silent prayer, hands clasped in front of him. He slid up beside him and whispered in his ear, "Why aren't you answering my calls, bro?"

Shivraj's eyes opened, looked at him sideways, before closing again, and resuming his prayers.

"Hey, what's the matter with you?" Sunil grabbed him by the arm, pulling him to his feet. Shivraj shook his arm free but said nothing, his eyes fixed on the goddess. Sunil turned him around and pushed him in the back, forcing him toward the front entrance and out of the temple, ignoring the glares from the other worshippers. Sunil had no time for religion. Religion was for the weak.

Once outside, Shivraj shook himself free. "Leave me alone."

Sunil looked at the dark circles around Shivraj's eyes, the two day's stubble on his chin. "What the fuck is the matter with you? You don't answer my calls, you didn't turn up last night? You know we were supposed to go to Rahul's party."

Shivraj's lip started quivering, and his eyes welled up. "I'm next, Sunil. I'm next," he sobbed quietly.

Sunil grabbed him by the arm and pushed him toward his Mercedes double-parked at the entrance. "Get inside," he opened the passenger door and shoved him inside. He walked around to the driver's side, got in, and looked across at Shivraj, slumped in the chair, whimpering.

"What the fuck are you talking about? Look at you, blubbering like a girl."

Shivraj looked up and sniffed. He fixed his eyes on Sunil. "I am next, Sunil. I am going to die. It's my karma. We should never have done what we did to that woman or that man. Now, I have to pay the price. I deserve it." He broke down again, sobbing away.

Sunil reached across, grabbed Shivraj by the shirt and pulled him toward him, his face inches from his own.

"Now you listen to me, you weak motherfucker. You are not going to die. It's not karma or any other religious bullshit. No one knows what we did, and no one will ever know unless you start running your mouth off. We got rid of the only witness. Now get a grip on yourself." He released Shivraj's shirt and sat back in his seat, fuming.

"You don't understand, Sunil. What we did was wrong. We have to pay for it. Anil and Manish already have. And now, it's my turn." Shivraj looked down, his hands shaking. He gripped his thighs to stop his hands trembling and looked up at Sunil again. "Yesterday there was a dead chicken on my jeep. This morning one of those Tantric dolls with a nail in it. It's a sign, Sunil. My time has come."

"You stupid superstitious fuck!" Sunil shook his head, exasperated. "Can't you see? Someone is doing this. Do you understand me? A person. A human being. Not one of your gods. Not karma. There's no such fucking thing. It's all made up to keep weak people like you in your place."

Shivraj just sobbed and continued staring into the footwell.

"Fuck this," said Sunil, and started the engine, pulling away from the temple with a screech of his tires. Shivraj might be next, but no motherfucker was going to get Sunil Patil.

52

J ohn followed at a distance. He had followed Shivraj from his house to the temple, then watched with interest as Sunil had turned up later, dragging Shivraj out, and pushing him into the car. He had seen the anger in Sunil's body language, but he had also seen the disintegration of Shivraj. He couldn't believe how fast his plan was working. The power of the human mind was an incredible thing. Shivraj was a quivering wreck of his former self. No longer the cocky aspiring politician, he had been reduced to a whimpering jelly in the space of two days, the destructive power of guilt and an irrational belief in superstition.

Sunil was something else though, John thought as he followed the Mercedes back to Shivnagar along the Sankey Tank Road. His anger was clearly visible, his arrogance showing no signs of disappearing. He would lash out soon, and John had better be ready. Time to step up his plans for Shivraj.

Nearing the turn for Sunil's street, he slowed, waiting until the Mercedes turned into the driveway before turning

onto the street. Nearing Sunil's gate, he slowed imperceptibly and glanced toward the house. Through the gap in the
closing gate, he saw Sunil at the passenger side of the
Mercedes hauling Shivraj out by the arm and pushing him
toward the front door. Shivraj stumbled, his head hung in
dejection.

John grinned, enjoying the self-destruction of his quarry
and increased his speed. He turned right at the corner and
drove away, swerving slightly to avoid a mound of builder's
waste spilling over the footpath and onto the road from an
under-construction block of apartments. Seeing the pile of
rubble, steel off-cuts, and discarded piping, John had
another idea.

53

unil kept Shivraj with him the whole day. He couldn't risk him roaming around, blabbing his mouth off. In his current state, he was bound to say anything, admit what he had done, and incriminate them all. Instead, Sunil wanted to keep an eye on him. Sunil's father was away in Delhi, so he had sent his father's driver to retrieve Shivraj's jeep from outside the temple and bring it home while he thought about what to do. Sunil looked over at Shivraj slumped in his chair, at the dark circles under his eyes, the unshaven face, and the unwashed hair. He shook his head. Idiot. He stood and walked out onto the fourth-floor landing.

"Sanju," he called out.

"Sir?" came the answer from downstairs.

"Bring two glasses and a bottle of Black Label."

"Yes, Sir."

Sunil sat back down and picked up a packet of cigarettes from the table, shaking one out. Lighting it, he took a long pull, holding the smoke in, allowing the nicotine to take hold before blowing it out in a long cloud. He sat back and thought while he waited for the whiskey. The fact a chicken and a voodoo doll had appeared in Shivraj's jeep pointed to human involvement. While Anil's and Manish's deaths could have been attributed to accidental and natural causes, something which Sunil had never quite believed, the latest developments meant someone was definitely involved. But who?

A knock on the door interrupted his thoughts, and Sanju, the house servant, came in with a half-full bottle of Black Label and two whiskey glasses on a tray. He placed it down on the table in front of Sunil and straightened up.

"Ice, Sir?"

"No."

Sanju turned and walked toward the door as Sunil twisted the top off the whiskey bottle.

"Sanju, one minute."

"Sir?"

Sunil stood, walked over to a cabinet at the side of the room, slid open a drawer, pulled out a Ziploc bag filled with ganja and a packet of cigarette papers. He tossed them over to Sanju who caught them in mid-air.

"Roll a couple of these."

"Yes, Sir." Sanju came over to the table, knelt on the floor and deftly rolled a couple of joints while Sunil splashed two large whiskeys into the glasses. He sat and waited until Sanju had finished, then dismissed him with a flick of his hand. He stood and walked around to Shivraj handing him a glass. Shivraj took it without looking up.

"Listen to me."

Shivraj reluctantly looked up at Sunil.

"This is not karma. This is not bad luck. This is someone fucking with your head, and you are stupid enough to believe it."

Shivraj shook his head, and his hand trembled, the whiskey glass shaking. "No, you don't understand. What we did was wrong. I know it now. We are being punished." He took a large gulp from the whiskey glass. "We have to make amends, Sunil."

Sunil took a deep breath, trying hard to contain his anger. He bent over Shivraj, his face now at the same level as his, just inches away.

"Now you listen to me." He raised his finger pointing straight at Shivraj. "No-one punishes us. We do whatever we want. My father is Surya Patil, and no one will mess with us. As long as you keep your fucking mouth shut."

Shivraj started sobbing, his whole body shaking.

Sunil stood exasperated, walked to the table, and lit one of the joints. He took a long puff then handed it to Shivraj. "Here finish this, it will calm you down."

Shivraj shook his head.

"I said finish it," growled Sunil.

Shivraj took it reluctantly and took a puff. He tried to hold it in but couldn't do so for long.

"Take another drag."

He took another, holding it in longer this time, his sobs slowing, his body shaking less, the effect of the cannabidiol binding with his serotonin receptors, calming him down as Sunil stood and watched.

It had been a risk, some people became more anxious instead of calmer after smoking a joint, but Sunil saw it was working on Shivraj.

"Another," he instructed. Shivraj took another, then offered the joint back to Sunil. Sunil shook his head, "Finish it." Sunil needed to keep his mind clear. He sat back down, picked up his whiskey glass, took a sip and watched Shivraj. He was becoming a liability.

54

I t was six p.m. by the time John was back, parked under the tree at the end of Sunil's street. It had taken John most of the day to finalize his preparations, but he now felt he was ready. The more he thought about Sunil's growing agitation, the more he realized time was running short for him to safely take action. He needed to do something before Sunil lashed out. It wasn't the route he preferred, but he realized he now had to get his hands dirty and get physical.

He glanced nervously toward the passenger footwell where he had stowed the items he would need for his plan. There was a piece of iron pipe about two feet long wrapped in newspaper and a black knitted woolen balaclava John had picked up earlier in the day from a sporting goods store. Beside it was a cloth banner from one of the opposing political parties which John had pulled down from a tree in one of the nearby streets. John's plan was to somehow catch Shivraj when he was alone and take advantage of his nervous state so Shivraj would not defend himself. Hopefully, this would allow John time to get in the first blow with the iron pipe and beat Shivraj to death. It was crude, and the details made John feel sick to the stomach, but it was all he could think of in the short time he had available. He planned to leave the banner lying nearby as a red herring to point suspicion at political rivals. Many of the politicians made use of underemployed youth and bad elements to do a lot of their political dirty work, and fights between party members were not an uncommon occurrence. John was dressed in black, and with the addition of the black bala-clava, he imagined the sight of him appearing in the dark-ness would—in Shivraj's hyper nervous state—scare the shit out of him. Shivraj wasn't much bigger than John, but John had never fought anyone before in his life and needed to use every advantage he could get. He reclined his chair slightly and settled in for a long wait. There was no guar-antee Shivraj was still at Sunil's house, but the sight of his jeep parked outside and the lack of any other ideas meant all he could do was wait.

55

A t around ten p.m., the gates swung open, and Sunil's white Mercedes pulled out onto the road, turning left down the street, heading away from John. John straightened up, started the engine, and waited until the Mercedes had turned the corner before pulling out behind him. He kept his distance to avoid being spotted, the lighter traffic at this time of the evening making it easier to follow than during the day. John followed the Mercedes down onto Sankey Tank Road where he expected Sunil to turn right and head toward the Golf Course and into town. He was surprised when the Mercedes turned left and headed north, past Palace Grounds and through the under-pass at Mekhri Circle toward the Hebbal Flyover. John followed, hanging back, keeping the distinctive rear lights of the Mercedes just in sight as it crossed the Hebbal Flyover and joined the elevated highway toward the International Airport. John began to worry about what he would do if Sunil was taking a flight. He couldn't follow him onto a plane. If he took a flight when would he get back? Would he come back? How would John find him? John's mind raced back and forth, working out all possible scenarios but couldn't think of a solution. Thirty minutes later, the Mercedes slowed for the toll booth. John took care to enter a different booth and scrambled in the coin tray for spare change with one eye on the Mercedes as it accelerated away. He handed over the money and waited impatiently for his receipt to be printed out and the barrier to rise before following. He breathed a sigh of relief as the Mercedes passed the turnoff for the airport and continued north toward Devanahalli. Fifteen minutes later, the car pulled off the main highway and onto the service road, then took a left toward Nandi Hill. John hung back, keeping another car and a pickup truck between him and the Mercedes. The Mercedes slowed after about ten kilometers and indicated right, pulling onto a narrow lane that disappeared into the darkness. John slowed too, wondering what Sunil was up to. He pulled to the left allowing the car behind him to pass, then rolled quietly toward the turning. He saw the red tail lights disappearing up the lane and not wanting to lose them, he also turned right, turning off his headlights and following along in the dark. Fortunately, the light from the moon was just enough for him to make out the edges of the road although he had to drive with considerable care. Ahead he saw the red tail lights suddenly became brighter as the car braked to a stop.

John pulled over to the side of the road on an open patch of gravel and turned the engine off. He watched to see if the car would move, but it sat there. The driver's door opened, and Sunil walked around to the passenger side. John grabbed the steel pipe and the balaclava from the footwell, and making sure the interior light was switched to off, carefully opened the door. He pulled the balaclava down over his face, pressed the door shut with a click, and keeping close to the side of the road, crept forwards. Maybe, just maybe, he could get rid of both of them at the same time.

56

Sunil had spent the afternoon drinking, smoking, and thinking. The more he thought about it, the more he realized he had to make a tough decision. Shivraj was a quivering wreck. Sunil made sure he kept drinking and kept supplying him with fresh joints, but they were becoming less and less effective. He would remain relatively calm for a while before descending into a state of self-recrimination as soon as the effects wore off. He kept telling Sunil how they had to confess, how they must atone for their sins. Sunil just nodded but inside he was fuming. Sunil could never allow that to happen. Shivraj had to be dealt with.

By the evening, Sunil's mind was made up, and he waited until his mother and the servants had gone to bed before grabbing Shivraj by the arm and guiding him out to the car. Shivraj was compliant, he didn't care what was happening, just mumbling to himself. Sunil drove north out of the city, needing to find a place where he wouldn't be disturbed. He looked over at Shivraj who was now half asleep in the seat beside him, a string of drool hanging from the corner of his mouth onto his shirt. He would miss the stupid guy, but there was no way Sunil was about to allow him to talk about what they had done. His father would also wonder what had happened to him, but his place in the Party would be taken by someone else before the week was over.

Pulling into a quiet lane, he drove away from the main road into the darkness. He looked in the rear-view mirror to ensure he wasn't followed, but at this time of the night, all the country folk were at home, the fields deserted. He braked and pulled to the side of the road, put the Mercedes in park and wound down his window, listening to the sounds of the night. It was silent, no one around. In the distance, a dog barked, but there was nothing else, just the ticking of the cooling engine and a light snore from Shivraj —the combined effects of the marijuana, alcohol, and the motion of the car putting him into a deep sleep.

He took a deep breath, opened his door, and got out. Taking another look around to make sure he wasn't observed, he walked around the back of the car and to the passenger door. He opened it and unbuckled Shivraj's seat-belt. Bending forward, he picked him up under the arms, pulled him out of the car. Shivraj stirred and mumbled but didn't wake. Sunil straightened his back, and looking over his shoulder, he stepped backward off the road, dragging Shivraj with him. The road was lined with a small earth berm covered in shrubs and undergrowth before dropping away again into a rough patch of overgrazed ground. Sunil looked around and in the light of the moon could make out a patch of scrub about fifteen meters away from the road. He walked backward to the scrub, dragging Shivraj, his head slumped on Sunil's chest, his arms hanging loosely, his dragging feet barely leaving a mark on the hard-packed ground. Hauling him behind the scrub, out of sight from the road, Sunil laid Shivraj down on the ground and looked down at him while he caught his breath. He took another look around and paused, listening. High overhead he could hear an aircraft heading for the airport, but otherwise, the countryside was silent. He stepped with one foot over Shivraj and squatted down. Leaning forward he pinned Shivraj's arms to the ground with his knees.

"I'm sorry my friend, but you need to keep your mouth shut," he said softly. With both hands, he grabbed him around the throat and squeezed. Shivraj's eyes flicked open, not sure what was happening and as he struggled for breath, his legs started kicking, and he tried to free his arms. Sunil squeezed tighter, the tendons in his arms standing out like cords. Shivraj was now fully awake, his mouth open, panic in his eyes. He bucked his body and kicked out, trying to throw Sunil off, but the full day of drinking and the copious amounts of weed he had smoked had weakened him. There was nothing he could do as Sunil pressed harder, squeezing his hands together with all his might until eventually, the struggling stopped. Sunil kept his hands around Shivraj's throat for a little longer and gradually let go, shaking out the cramp in his arms. He observed the body for a moment, making sure he was dead, then stood, brushing the dust from his knees and straightened his shirt. He turned, and without looking back at his friend, he walked through the darkness to his car. Getting in, he started the Mercedes, put it in drive, took a U-turn, and headed back down the lane to the main road. The headlights picked up an SUV parked on the side of the road. It hadn't been there before, and he slowed down to see if there was anyone inside. It was empty. He frowned and drove on, reaching the main road and turning left to head back to Bangalore.

57

John curled himself into a ball, making himself as small as possible as he burrowed into the undergrowth beside the road. He was confident, in his black clothes, he wouldn't be spotted, but he wasn't willing to take a chance. He turned his face away from the car and stayed as still as he could as the Mercedes drove past. Shit! The car slowed down as it passed his SUV, and John mentally kicked himself for parking the vehicle where it could be seen. He held his breath, waiting for the car to stop but breathed a sigh of relief as it continued on. Once the car reached the end of the road and turned, he stood up and looked around.

John was puzzled by what he had seen. He had watched as Sunil had dragged Shivraj from the car and disappeared into the undergrowth. Sunil had returned a few minutes later alone. What had happened to Shivraj? John was pretty sure it wasn't good.

He walked toward where he had seen Sunil disappear, scanning the ground for clues, the steel pipe held ready in his hand, in case Shivraj jumped out on him. Fortunately, there was just enough ambient light for him to see, the sky being clear and the moon not far off full.

He neared the patch of scrub and walked behind it, having no trouble identifying the dark shape spread out on the ground. Taking care not to scuff the ground and leave any signs, he approached cautiously, holding the pipe ready although he sensed he wouldn't find Shivraj alive. He observed the body for a moment, checking for signs of movement, but there was nothing. Kneeling down, he placed his fingers on the side of Shivraj's neck and felt for a pulse—nothing. He was dead alright. John sat back on his heels and thought about what to do next. In a way, he was relieved Sunil had done the job for him. But he still felt uneasy when confronted with a dead body. Anil had been an accident, and he hadn't seen the result of his actions with Manish. But Shivraj was lying dead at his feet, and although he hadn't committed the murder himself, he was still involved. Seeing the body made it harder for him to disconnect. He stood carefully, brushing the dust off his knees. Still, he had to toughen up and put any conscience to one side if he was to complete what he had set out to do.

With one last glance back at the body, he turned and headed back to his vehicle.

Only one left to go.

58

I t was another three days before he got the expected knock on the door. Inspector Rajiv stood on the top step, a grim look on his face.

"Mr. Hayes, John, good morning."

"Rajiv, please come in." John stood to one side. He felt relaxed despite knowing the questions that were bound to follow. He knew he could safely deny the killing without any feelings of guilt. After all, he hadn't done it himself.

Rajiv walked inside shaking John's hand as he passed, then waited until John closed the door and walked past him toward the kitchen. John looked over his shoulder.

"I've just made a fresh pot of coffee, would you like some?"

"Yes, that will be nice, thank you."

Rajiv sat down at the kitchen bench while John found a mug and poured from the French press. "Milk, sugar?"

"Both, please."

John passed him the sugar and took a carton of milk from the fridge and placed it on the counter. He topped up his own mug and sat on the barstool next to Rajiv, taking a sip as Rajiv stirred three teaspoons of sugar into the mug and splashed some milk on top. He took a sip, licked his lips, then turned to face John.

"I need to ask you some official questions, John."

"Okay."

"What were you doing three days ago, John?"

"I was at home. Why?" John asked, frowning for authenticity.

Rajiv nodded and took another sip from his coffee mug.

"My colleagues in the Chikballapur District, north of here, found a body near Nandi Hill yesterday."

John said nothing, sipped his coffee, his eyes on Rajiv's face.

"The body had been partially eaten by stray dogs and birds, but we were able to identify it as belonging to Mr. Shivraj Gowda. Is the name familiar, John?"

"No, not at all."

"Well, he happens to be one of the men whose photo you had shown me previously. One of those you said was involved in your wife's death."

John nodded, still watching Rajiv's face. "How did he die?"

"He was murdered, John. Strangled and dumped in a field. A child from the village found the body on the way to school."

John pulled a face. "I can honestly say it had nothing to do with me, Rajiv. But as I have said before, if this man was involved, he deserved what happened to him."

Rajiv studied John's face for a moment, then looked down at the counter. He hesitated for a moment as if making a decision, then looked up again.

"Yes, perhaps you are right, but this is a murder case, and it won't be long before difficult questions start being asked. There have been three deaths in the past few weeks, all people in the same circle. Admittedly, the previous two have been explained away as an accident and natural causes, but this one is messier. Someone is going to start poking around, and I would hate for anyone to start pointing fingers in your direction. You have been through enough already, John."

John nodded. "I can't think why anybody would point their fingers at me Rajiv. I am an honest, law-abiding citizen, and these deaths, although in my eyes well deserved, have absolutely nothing to do with me."

Rajiv drained the rest of his coffee and stood. "Yes, John. As I thought." He extended his hand. "Thank you for the coffee."

John stood and shook his hand, and they both walked to the front door. Rajiv walked outside, stopped, and turned back toward John.

"The Patil family is one of the most powerful families in this state, John. They protect their own. I would be exceedingly careful if I was in your position." He paused, looking out at the neighboring houses before turning back and fixing John in his gaze. "In fact, if I was you, I would move my departure date forward. Why do you need to stay here? Go back to your country, John. Live a safe and comfortable life." With that, he turned and headed to his vehicle.

John watched as Rajiv pulled away in his Bolero and breathed a sigh of relief. Although he felt Rajiv was on his side, he couldn't be a hundred percent relaxed when he was around. Plus, he knew Rajiv was right. If Sunil could kill his own friend without compunction, it would only be a matter of time before he suspected John of being behind the deaths of Anil and Manish, and he would think nothing of taking him out of the picture. He had to be very careful from now on, but he also needed to act fast and hit Sunil before Sunil hit him.

John was looking forward to some closure. He wanted to complete his revenge and get out of the country. There were too many memories in the house. He needed to get out and start life anew, somewhere where the memories would not be so hurtful. But first, he had to complete the promise he had made to himself and to Charlotte. He would avenge her death—of that he was certain.

59

B ack at the station, Rajiv was immediately called into the Senior Police Inspector's office.

"What's happening on the Shivraj Gowda case?" The SPI asked before Rajiv had a chance to sit down.

"Sir, we are continuing our investigation. Thanks to our colleagues in Chikballapur District, we know the cause of death, the approximate time of death, but we don't know what he was doing there, and we have yet to establish his movements leading up to his death. Anyway, Sir, it's not in my jurisdiction. Chikballapur should be investigating."

"That's all changed now, Rajiv. The case has been transferred here. Mr. Gowda was a prominent member of the PPA. I don't need to tell you how much pressure is coming to bear on me from up high. Surya Patil has personally called me to make sure we are looking after the issue."

Rajiv nodded in apparent understanding. Inside though, he was boiling. No-one was interested when Mrs. Hayes was murdered. The system stank. There was justice only for those with power.

"Yes, Sir. I will have my best men look into it." He stood. "Is there anything else, Sir?"

"That will be all, Rajiv," he paused. "But Rajiv..."

"Yes, Sir?"

"I want results and fast."

"Of course, Sir."

60

Sunil had kept to himself since Shivraj's death, staying at home, not venturing out. The days passed in a blur of whiskey and nicotine. Twice his mother had asked him if everything was okay, a look of concern in her eyes. She was used to his drinking and partying and had long ago given up trying to correct him, but even she had noticed a change in his demeanor. His father though, true to form, had paid him little attention upon his return from Delhi, more interested in trying to find out who had killed Shivraj, convinced one of his political rivals was out to get at him. Sunil had panicked when that corrupt slug Muniappa from the Shivnagar Police Station had appeared at the house, but relaxed when he heard his father berating him over his lack of results. Sunil had nothing to worry about with regard to Shivraj, but he still had to find out who was behind the black magic. Someone knew, and Sunil wouldn't be safe until he too was disposed of.

That afternoon Sunil was already halfway through a bottle of Black Label when there was a knock on his door.

"What is it?" he growled.

The door opened slightly, and Sanju poked his head in. "Sir, an Inspector Sampath is downstairs asking to see you."

Shit! Sampath, Sampath, the name didn't ring a bell. He wasn't one of the cops Sunil usually dealt with. Besides, Muniappa had told his father the police had no leads. Who the fuck was this guy? Why has he come to me and not my father? Am I a suspect? Shit! Fuck!

"Is he alone?"

"Yes, Sir."

"Okay, I'll be down in a minute."

"Sir."

Sunil took a deep breath and drained the contents of his glass. He stubbed out his cigarette and stood, mentally composing himself. If the cop was alone, he probably hadn't come to arrest him. If he did arrest him, Sunil knew he would be out within the hour. It should be okay. He must have just come to ask some questions. Yes, that's it. He had to behave normally, be above suspicion. He exhaled, expelling all the tension built up in his body. Everything would be okay. Opening the door, he walked out and headed downstairs.

61

Rajiv sat uncomfortably on the edge of an overstuffed chair in the large living room and looked around at the ostentatious furniture, the expensive ornaments, the framed pictures of Surya Patil shaking hands with dignitaries and VIPs. Quite an achievement to accumulate all this and certainly not possible on a humble Minister's salary. What did they officially take home? Forty-thousand rupees a month? Not enough to pay for a house this size, let alone the fleet of foreign cars, and who knew what other properties he owned? Surya Patil was a successful businessman but Rajiv was sure his wealth was not all legitimate. The system was so far gone, the politicians didn't even make any attempt to hide the evidence of the corruption. It was so blatant. It was almost accepted the best route to rapid accumulation of immense wealth was through politics.

Rajiv's thoughts were interrupted as Sunil walked into the room. He stood and proffered his hand, but Sunil ignored him and sat down in the chair opposite him.

"What can I do for you, Inspector?"

Rajiv hesitated, noting the arrogance, the word 'Inspector' said almost as an afterthought. He sat back down, perching himself on the edge of the chair. He looked Sunil over—his unshaven jaw, the dark circles around his eyes, his disheveled appearance. Rajiv had not met the man before but had seen plenty of photos and had also seen him from afar at political gatherings. He had never seen him look this unkempt, and he reeked of booze and stale cigarette smoke.

Rajiv cleared his throat. "I believe you have heard about the death of Mr. Shivraj Gowda?"

"Yes, I have."

"He was a friend of yours?"

"More of an acquaintance. He did a lot of work for my father."

Rajiv nodded, making a mental note of the term Sunil used.

"Mr. Gowda was last seen at the Meenakshi Temple five days ago."

"I hear he liked to pray," Sunil replied, examining his fingernails.

"You don't seem very upset, Mr. Patil?"

"It's an unfortunate thing, but I told you, he was just an acquaintance."

Rajiv nodded and pursed his lips. He leaned forward in the chair. "The thing is Mr. Patil, eyewitnesses mention that he left the temple with a man matching your description, in a white Mercedes, just like the one parked outside."

Sunil shrugged. "Ah yes, that's right, I forgot. My father asked me to pick him up and bring him here."

"Is that normal Mr. Patil? Couldn't he have asked one of his staff to do that?"

"Yes, he could have, but I think they were busy that morning."

"And why did your father need him?"

Sunil glared at Rajiv. "I have no idea. Why don't you ask him? Will there be anything else, Inspector?"

"Just a couple more questions, Mr. Patil. What did Mr. Gowda do after you brought him to the house?"

"I told you, my father wanted to see him."

"What time was that, Mr. Patil? What time did he leave?"

Sunil shrugged, irritation showing on his face. "I don't know, maybe mid-afternoon. Look, I'm a busy man, Inspector. Why don't you go out and investigate? Find out who killed him instead of wasting my time." Sunil stood up.

Rajiv also stood, the interview evidently over. "Mr. Patil, thank you for your time. Please be assured, I will not rest until I find out what happened."

Sunil frowned and studied Rajiv, looking him up and down as if thinking how to respond. He then turned and walked out the door, calling out, "Sanju, show the Inspector out."

Rajiv walked out to his vehicle. He knew Sunil was lying. The story didn't match up with the timings. If he had picked up Shivraj in the morning why did he leave in the afternoon? What was he doing all that time? Muniappa had told him Surya Patil had been in Delhi, so it wasn't possible he had wanted to see Shivraj. Another thing he didn't understand was why Sunil said Shivraj was just an acquaintance when pictures of the two together had been posted numerous times in the society pages of the newspapers? None of it made any sense. More and more he believed that John Hayes had nothing to do with this murder, and his other theory—that Shivraj had been murdered by a political rival—was also starting to look implausible. Sunil Patil had jumped to the top of the suspect list. But why would he kill his friend?

62

John sat in the deck chair, looking out across the garden as the sun's gentle rays filtered through the branches of the frangipani trees. He loved the early mornings in India. The light was soft, the temperature cool, and there was a tranquility which could not be found once the population of over a billion people started their day. A koel called out from a neighboring garden, its distinctive *koo-ei koo-ei* call a sound he would forever associate with his time here. In the branches just above him, a tiny Silver-Eye cheeped to its partner before both of them darted across to a tree on the other side of the garden. John sipped from his mug of black coffee, savoring the taste of the single estate blend of robusta and arabica he had picked up from an estate in the coffee-growing region of Chikmagalur. It was without the chicory that was usually added to South Indian Filter Coffee, John preferring his coffee unadulterated. Memories of that trip came back to him as he stared out across the garden.

It had been a wonderful holiday in a beautiful bed-and-breakfast, surrounded by coffee plants and shade trees filled with wildlife. The fresh air, the peace and quiet, and long relaxing walks through the plantation were the perfect antidote to their busy lives in the city. On one of their walks, they were startled as a wild boar burst out from the undergrowth onto the path in front of them, Charlotte grabbing his arm in fear, then giggling with delight as the sow's piglets trotted out after it. Their life in India together had been wonderful, but there were too many memories. Experiences which sadly could never be repeated. John didn't think he would ever return, at least to this part of the country and had already booked his return flight to England in four days' time. He took another sip of coffee and watched as a pair of eagles circled in the sky high above, spiraling higher and higher in the thermal updraft until they were no longer visible to the naked eye. John's imminent departure also meant he had to complete his final act of vengeance. This last one would be the toughest and was another reason why he had booked the flight. If he hadn't, he would drag it out, procrastinating and postponing what had to be done.

The problem was he still didn't know how to do it. Sunil was a far different prospect to the others. He was bigger, tougher, more aggressive, and with his father's bodyguard regularly at the house, often better protected than the others had been. He was also on edge and aware someone was after him, now that the others had died. John knew he would have to be extra careful, not only to avoid being caught but also to avoid being killed himself. If he hadn't already done so, it wouldn't take long for Sunil to put two and two together and realize John was behind it all.

John closed his eyes and leaned his head against the back of the chair. He pictured Charlotte in his mind, drawing strength from her image although it was becoming more difficult, her image fading more and more with the passing of each day.

He shouldn't worry, he reasoned. The universe had looked after him so far. He hadn't known how to kill the others when he started, but now they were all dead. What had seemed impossible a matter of weeks ago, had happened successfully. He, John Hayes, an office manager from England, a man who had never been in a fight let alone harmed anyone, had killed two people and got away with it. He would have murdered the third, but fate had once again stepped in and helped him out. He was sure a way to complete his revenge would present itself before long.

John stood up and stretched. One thing was for sure though. It wouldn't present itself to him while he was sitting at home. He needed to follow Sunil again.

63

An hour later, John was sitting in his usual place, slumped out of sight in the back seat, a flask of hot coffee and a paper bag filled with samosas on the seat beside him. He settled in for another long day of watching and waiting.

By eleven o'clock the coffee was finished and most of the samosas eaten. He had peed twice into an empty plastic water bottle and wished he had kept another one handy. Before then, no one had left the house, people only going in, but finally, John saw the gate open, and Sunil's white Mercedes C Class poked its nose out onto the street before turning and heading down the road in John's direction. John slumped down to avoid being seen as the Mercedes approached, and tensed as he heard the engine note decrease. The car appeared to be slowing, and he started to panic but relaxed again as it continued on down the road before slowing for the junction and turning right. John tentatively raised his head and looked back to make sure the car had gone before jumping out and climbing into the driver's seat. He started the car and after a quick U-turn followed the Mercedes.

64

Sunil pulled out of his driveway and turned right down the street. His mood was foul, his head heavy with the after-effects of a full bottle of whiskey, and his mouth felt like the bottom of a birdcage. He had snapped at the staff before leaving and ignored his mother as she came to wish him good morning. As he pulled out of the gate and into the street, he thought over the events of the past couple of weeks. He had lost three of his friends, and although Sunil didn't like to admit it, he was lonely. Drinking wasn't the same without his friends to tease and joke around with, to pester girls, and make lewd comments. In fact, he hadn't been out for the last week, instead holing up in his rooms on the top floor of the house. But sitting around at home feeling sorry for himself had got to him, and today, he decided to go out and get a haircut and a shave, a bit of pampering to make himself feel better.

As he neared the end of the street, an SUV caught his eye. Something about it triggered a memory, and he slowed to take a closer look. It was a white Mahindra Scorpio SUV, the same model and color as the one he had seen parked on the side of the road the night he had killed Shivraj. There was no one in the car. Perhaps it was a coincidence, it was a fairly common vehicle, and there were many of the same color in the city, but still, a nagging feeling lingered in the back of his brain. He drove on uneasily—he didn't like coincidences. He wished he had taken note of the registration number that night. He shook his head. Forget it. He was becoming weak and paranoid like Shivraj.

Turning right at the end of the street, he headed down toward Sankey Tank Road, slowing for the junction at the bottom and indicated left. Out of habit, he looked in his rear-view, mirror and there, back at the end of the road, he saw the same SUV turn onto the street. He frowned, tensing up, his fingers tightening on the steering wheel. He turned left and followed the road down onto the underpass and up the other side toward Windsor Manor Circle before looking in the mirror again. It was still there, far back, almost hidden in the traffic. Sunil had to search for it, but the white SUV was there. He continued on past the Golf Course, taking a left, then a right past the police commissioner's office, all the time one eye on his rear-view mirror, the SUV always just in sight. He drove on past the cricket stadium, crossing MG Road and down toward Vittal Mallya Road where he turned right toward U. B. City. He pulled into the parking entrance and waited while the mall security completed their cursory security check. Idiots, Sunil thought, as the staff simply opened the trunk and glanced inside before waving him on. It would be so easy to smuggle weapons into the building with these useless security guards.

He drove into the parking building, finding a spot on the ground floor level near the entrance, then turned off the engine and waited. A few minutes later, the white SUV entered the parking and cruised slowly past before driving up the ramp to the next level. With the poor light in the parking area, Sunil couldn't quite make out the driver. Maybe it was all a coincidence? Maybe he was getting paranoid? There were plenty of white SUVs in the city. Maybe it was just chance that one from Shivnagar was also coming to U. B. City on the same day. Sunil opened the door and got out. He needed to be careful though. He needed to find out more. If it was the same vehicle that was there that night, it was possible the driver knew what had happened. He couldn't take the chance. He jogged across the parking and up the ramp to the next level, pausing halfway up, his head at the level of the next floor, and scanned the parking bays looking for the vehicle. There it was in the far corner, the driver just climbing out and with a beep, locking the door. Sunil ran up the remainder of the ramp and ducked down behind a Toyota sedan as the driver walked toward the entrance to the mall. Sunil watched him through the Toyota windows, still not quite able to see who it was, and when the driver disappeared inside the mall, he stood and hurried over to the entrance.

65

John cursed himself as he parked the SUV on the second level of parking. He had spotted the Mercedes parked near the entrance and in his peripheral vision had seen Sunil still sitting in the car. It had been too close. He hadn't expected him to still be in the vehicle or parked so close to the entrance. John didn't know why he had been so stupid as to follow him into the mall. There was nothing he could do in such a crowded place, no way an opportunity would ever present itself to him there. No, he had to concentrate, be more careful, pay attention to the details. There was no way he could allow himself to fail this close to the end. John turned off the engine and climbed out of the car. He locked it and walked across the parking bays to the mall entrance. He wouldn't waste time trying to watch Sunil in the mall, but he could at least use the toilets. Peeing into a bottle wasn't his idea of fun.

John ignored the fancy window displays of the watch boutiques and the shops selling high-end fashion and followed the signs for the W.C. He found the door to the men's toilet, the attendant deep in conversation outside with the ladies' toilet attendant. Ignoring them, he walked past and pushed the door open. The toilet was empty, and as was his habit, he headed for the furthest urinal and unzipped his pants. He closed his eyes in relief as his bladder emptied itself. He was sick of spending his days hiding in his car, fueled by cold food and coffee. He was looking forward to it all being over, to living a normal life again. Not long now.

He was almost done when he sensed, rather than felt, a movement near him but before he could open his eyes, he was shoved violently sideways. Caught by surprise, he hit the wall and fell to the floor, urine splashing on his pant legs. He couldn't see his attacker but felt a pair of hands grabbing him, one by his hair and the other by his shirt, dragging him across the toilet floor into one of the cubicles. He was dumped on the floor, his face just millimeters away from the commode.

"Hey, what the fuck!" he turned his head, looked up, and a cold shaft of fear ran through him, paralyzing his body. His attacker delivered a swift kick to John's stomach, and he curled up in pain, retching and gasping for breath. He felt the hot breath on his face, and the stench of stale nicotine as Sunil knelt down beside him.

"Why are you following me, you motherfucker?"

John curled himself smaller, fearing another blow but also attempting to keep his face hidden. He still clung on to the hope Sunil didn't know who he was. Struggling for breath he swallowed back the pain, thinking fast.

"What are you t-t-t-talking about?" he stammered. "I'm doing some shopping."

"You were following me. You followed me from Shivnagar!" Sunil grabbed his face with one hand and turned it toward him, staring at him, memorizing his face.

"I live in Shivnagar," John lied. "I always come to U. B. City for shopping and to have lunch."

"What's your address then?"

"It's none of your business. Who do you think you are?"

Sunil slapped him in the face, John's eyes smarting and his cheek turning red with the blow.

"What's your address?" he growled.

John thought frantically. He didn't know the street names, but he had to say something. Guessing the names were fairly generic, he made up an address, hoping Sunil would believe him.

"4th Cross, No. 53."

Sunil stood up straight and stared down at him, hesitating, as if not knowing what to do next

They both heard the main toilet door opening, and someone walked in. Sunil glared at John.

"You had better not be lying," he muttered, then cleared his throat and spat on him, the side of John's face hit by a large globule of saliva. Sunil turned, kicked John's legs out of the way, pulled the cubicle door open, and walked out, pulling the door shut behind him.

John lay there catching his breath, then grimaced as he realized he had been lying on a toilet floor. He grabbed the edge of the commode and pulled himself up, then flipped down the toilet seat and sat down. With a piece of toilet paper, he wiped the spittle from his face and tucked in his shirt, wincing at the pain in his abdomen. He probed his ribs with his fingers, but they were okay. He sat back and contemplated his next move. Things had definitely stepped up a level.

66

From the toilets, Sunil went straight to the parking area, snapping a picture of the SUV's number plates with his phone before jumping into his car and heading out of the carpark, his haircut and shave appointment forgotten. Even with his influence, he wasn't keen to hang around and answer any questions if the expat had called the police. He turned right onto Vittal Mallya Road, then drove across the junction into Cubbon Park, driving through the grounds and woodlands until he found an empty parking space. He pulled in and grabbed his phone. A parking attendant approached the car, and Sunil snarled at him through the window, the attendant beating a hasty retreat, an argument with an angry rich thug not worth his meager salary. Sunil thumbed through the address book on his phone until he found the number he wanted and then pressed dial.

It rang three times before it was answered. "Yes, Sir?"

"Ravi, I'm sending you on WhatsApp a number plate. I want you to find out who owns the car."

"Yes, Sir."

"Quickly Ravi. It's urgent."

"I will do it right away, Sir."

Sunil hung up. It was always handy to have a policeman on retainer, you never knew when it would come in useful. He sat there thinking, looking out across the gardens, oblivious to the scenes in front of him, the children running in the grass, the trees filled with parrots. Instead, a movie of recent events flickered through his head. Maybe the man was innocent? A lot of expats did live in Shivnagar, and they all went shopping from time to time in U. B. City. It was a popular destination. But he needed to know for sure, and he had a nagging feeling he had seen this guy before. With Constable Ravi's help, he would get to the bottom of it.

Sunil was uncharacteristically worried. The address the expat had given him hadn't checked out, and it had only taken a day for Constable Ravi to find out who the car was registered to. When he heard the name, Sunil had felt sick. It had all finally made sense—the deaths of Anil and Manish, Shivraj's well-founded paranoia. Someone had been targeting them all along. Sunil was the only one left.

Like all bullies, Sunil thrived on taking advantage of people weaker than him. He always had, and it had been easy. No one ever fought back or complained. His family was richer than most and held so much power even the police turned a blind eye to his misbehavior. No-one ever dared to object when he pushed his way around. No-one ever dared to complain when he and his friends had misbehaved in restaurants and bars or assaulted young women on drunken nights out. If anyone had even tried to register a complaint, the police, hearing his name, would always refuse to file a report, instead telling the victims not to bother. Admittedly, with the foreign woman, he had gone a bit far. The boys had got carried away. They hadn't planned to kill her when they dragged her from the car, but he had realized, after their lust was spent and they had sobered up a little, even Sunil's father wouldn't be able to get them out of this one. She had to go. Dead people don't complain, and he had been right. It had all died down, been forgotten, old news. Until a couple of weeks ago.

That motherfucking husband of hers! Who did he think he was? Why was he even still in the country? Sunil's friends were all dead, and he knew he was next on the list. He had to kill the bastard at the earliest opportunity.

67

John was hunkered down in the back of a rented red Hyundai hatchback, watching Sunil's house. He hadn't wanted to take the chance Sunil would recognize his white SUV again. It had taken most of the morning to work out how to disable the GPS tracker from the hire car, but finally, thanks to a YouTube video, he discovered it only required the removal of a fuse. John wanted no record of his movements. Since midday, he had been on the street outside Sunil's house but not seen anything of interest. There had been plenty of visitors but no sign of Sunil. His flask of coffee was empty, and he had eaten the last of his sandwiches half an hour ago. He would be happy when these long days cramped in the back of a car would be over. Removing his wallet from his back pocket, he opened it and looked at the passport photo of Charlotte he kept tucked into the clear plastic sleeve. Tears welled up in his eyes.

"Not long now, Charlotte. Only one left." He kissed the photo and flipped the wallet shut before slipping it back into his pocket. His resolve reinforced, he settled in for a few more hours of watching.

By seven p.m., he had almost given up on any chance of seeing Sunil that day. The traffic in and out of the house had reduced significantly, and the street was quiet, bathed in the yellow glow from the street lamps. Now and then, a car would pull into one of the neighboring houses as the owners returned, but there was no foot traffic. The pack of stray dogs at the end of the street barked and squabbled, disturbing the crows sleeping in the tree overhead, the birds making their displeasure known with a chorus of angry caws. John yawned and stretched, easing the stiffness in his back and legs. He pressed his stomach gingerly, still sore from Sunil's kicking. It had been a long fruitless day, and he wanted to go home. His head throbbed with a dull headache, and he closed his eyes to ease the strain from a day spent staring at the house. A wave of drowsiness come over him, the caffeine from his flask of coffee long since worn off.

It was more a sixth sense rather than any sound that alerted him. He opened his eyes with a start and turned, but it was already too late. The rear passenger door was wrenched open, and the next thing he knew, he was staring down the barrel of a gun.

68

Sunil had spotted him earlier in the afternoon. From the front window of his suite of rooms on the top floor of the house, most of the street was visible, and if he stood to the far left of the window, he could see right to the end of the street. It had become his habit in the last couple of days since assaulting John Hayes to watch the street for any sign of the white SUV. It hadn't returned, but today, in the space under the tree where he had last seen the SUV, was a red Hyundai with the black and yellow number plates of a rental car. He had taken the pair of binoculars he normally used for staring into his neighbor's daughter's bedroom, and standing back from the window to avoid being seen, examined the car closely. On first glance, there appeared to be no one in it, both the front seats empty. He ignored it the first time. But two hours later he saw the car hadn't moved and scanned it with the binoculars again. As he watched, the car moved as someone shifted their weight inside. There was someone in the back seat. A wave of anger rose in the pit of his stomach. Maybe his paranoia was getting the better of him, maybe it was just someone's driver catching up on sleep in the back seat, a common sight in Bangalore, but he wasn't prepared to take a chance. If that motherfucker was spying on him again, he would make sure it was the last time he spied on anyone. He was the son of Surya Patil, and no white-skinned bastard was going to get the better of him. It was going to end and end today.

Grabbing a bottle of Black Label and a glass, he moved his chair to the window, poured himself a generous shot, and settled in to wait. He was reluctant to do anything during the day, there was too much chance of being seen. He would wait until it got dark, then take action.

69

By nightfall, the car still hadn't moved. He had been watching it for a couple of hours and had seen the car shift imperceptibly once or twice. The rear window was slightly open too, proving there was, in fact, someone in the rear seat. By now, Sunil was halfway through the bottle of Black Label, and the more he drank, the angrier he got. Turning from the window, he crossed the room and opened his wardrobe. On the top shelf, out of sight and reach of the servants, was a shoebox. He removed it, and lifting the lid, he pulled out a handgun. It was an American made Walther PPK/S with the extended beavertail, and it was chambered for .32 caliber. The magazine held eight rounds which were more than enough for what he planned. Sunil had bought it on the black market a year ago. He could have bought it legally with a license, the .32 caliber being a non-prohibited bore in India, but that would have meant letting his father know with all the questions that would have entailed. It was much easier to get it illegally. He had never had to fire it in anger, he and his friends only shooting cans in a field one drunken evening. The rest of the time he just waved it around for show, the mere sight of it enough to frighten most people. It would come in very useful tonight. He checked the safety was on and tucked it into the waistband of his jeans, pulling his shirt over the top. He poured another generous shot of Black Label into his glass and drained it in one large gulp, the fire of the whiskey filling his belly. He was ready.

Sunil jogged downstairs and ducked out the back door. The boundary wall between his house and the house it backed onto wasn't high, and it was an easy climb for Sunil. He dropped to the other side and ran along the path between the house and the side wall. He wasn't too worried about being spotted. The house hadn't been occupied for the past month; the owners ran a business in Bahrain and divided their time between the two countries. Getting out onto the street was a little more difficult though as the main gate was locked from the outside and the front wall was almost six feet high and topped with broken glass. There was a smaller steel access door to the side, and when he looked closer, he saw it was unlocked but bolted from the inside. He slipped the bolt and looked both ways before walking out onto the street, turning left to head toward the corner. At the junction, he took another left, then it was one more left turn into his street. Before turning, he paused and peered around the wall at the corner to ensure he wouldn't be spotted. The street was empty, but he heard a car approaching from behind, so he pulled out his phone, pretending to study the screen as the car drove past. Once it reached the end of the street, he set off, keeping close to the line of parked cars, stepping carefully to avoid making any noise. A stray dog looked up at him nervously before running across the road.

As he neared the car, he could just make out the top of

someone's head leaning back against the seat. After a quick look up and down the street, he reached behind him and pulled the Walther from his waistband. Approaching slowly and quietly, he took a deep breath and with his left hand, yanked open the passenger door and pointed the pistol at the man inside. Just as he thought. It wasn't a driver.

"You again, you motherfucker. John fucking Hayes!" he snarled.

70

J ohn put his hands up and slid back against the side door, trying to put as much distance as he could between himself and the gun. How the fuck had Sunil got out of the house without being seen? How had he known he was here? John felt the adrenaline kick in, his hands shaking, his heart pounding. He looked from the gun to Sunil's face, could smell the alcohol on his breath, could see the fury in his eyes. For the second time since this began, he felt really afraid.

"We are going for a drive. Get in the front seat. Don't even think about doing anything stupid because I will shoot you like a fucking dog."

John thought fast. He could try running, but that would invite a bullet in the back. In the state Sunil was in, he wouldn't think twice about shooting him. He would have to do what he said and look for an opportunity to escape later.

"Okay, okay. I'm just opening the door." John hesitantly moved his hand to the door and opened it. Sunil watched him closely, keeping the gun pointed at John's center of mass. John stepped out carefully, closed the door, and moved to the front. Sunil was now pointing the gun at him over the roof of the car, unafraid of being seen. His eyes were red, and he was breathing heavily. John opened the front door and sat on the driver's seat. Sunil sat in the back, closed the door, and slid across behind John, jabbing him in the side with the gun barrel. He snarled in John's ear, flecks of spittle spraying John's neck.

"Drive!"

John started the car, pulled out into the road, and moved down the street, gradually increasing speed. Sunil directed him out onto the main road, and they headed north out of the city along the Airport Road.

"I should have known it was you. You killed Anil and Manish, didn't you?"

John said nothing, just glanced in the mirror at Sunil, not wanting to make him any angrier.

Sunil jabbed him in the ribs. "Answer me!"

John winced, his midsection still sore. "Yes, I killed them, and I would have killed Shivraj too, but you beat me to it."

"You fucker," Sunil slapped him on the head with his left hand, causing John to swerve, setting off a round of honking from the cars behind. John straightened the car and looked in the mirror, catching Sunil's eyes with his own, his fear replaced with anger.

"You are next."

"You think you can kill me?" Sunil laughed. "I'm the one with the gun. You are going to die, motherfucker. I will make sure it's a slow painful death, and then I'll leave you to rot in the sun just like I did with that whore of a wife of yours." Sunil leaned forward until his lips were close to John's ear.

"She was good, we all enjoyed her. We made her squeal like a pig."

John's fingers tightened on the wheel, his eyes filled with angry tears. Even if it meant losing his own life, he would make sure his face would be the last face Sunil would ever see.

71

They followed the airport road north, past the turning for John's house, passing Yelahanka and on toward the Airport. The same route Sunil had taken when he had killed Shivraj. John ran over all the options in his mind. It didn't take long. He didn't have any. There was a gun stuck in his side, a gun held by a crazy drunk killer who felt he was untouchable. John thought of Inspector Rajiv, but there was no way he could alert him. He had deliberately left his phone at home so the police couldn't track him. He was on his own.

Strangely enough, though, he no longer felt scared. It was as if everything he had worked toward since coming back to India was coming to a climax. He would finally get closure, one way or the other. He settled back into his seat, calmer, eyes on the road but occasionally flicking to the rear-view mirror to watch Sunil. Sunil didn't say much apart from giving John directions, the gun no longer held to John's side but resting on Sunil's lap. John noticed Sunil wasn't wearing a seatbelt, and he contemplated ramming the car into a wall, but the more he thought about it, the more he realized it wasn't a good idea. He would have difficulty explaining why Sunil was in his rental car, and besides, with Sunil's finger on the trigger, John didn't like the idea of stray bullets flying around the car. He had seen Pulp Fiction. He would wait for the right moment.

Thirty minutes later, Sunil instructed John to turn off the highway and take the service road which they followed for half a kilometer before Sunil told him to take a left turn. John slowed, turning onto a much narrower country road, unlit by street lights. He followed it for about three kilometers before Sunil told him to stop beside a large hoarding advertising a new development of luxury villas. Sunil opened the window and listened, his eyes scanning the entrance. There was no one around, not even a watchman. He made John turn into the entrance and follow the road as it wound its way between the vacant sites and partially completed homes. His headlights picked up a cow lying in the middle of the road, and it looked at them curiously as John slowed the car and negotiated his way around it. Sunil peered out the window, looking for something. John drove on until Sunil told him to stop beside an almost completed villa toward the far end of the development. They were now well away from the main road, and behind the villa, the estate looked out onto open farmland. John turned off the engine and waited for instructions. Sunil looked out the window at the house, the gun still pointed in John's direction. He turned to John.

"Give me the keys."

John took them out of the ignition, handed them back, and Sunil pocketed them.

"Get out of the car and walk around to the house."

John opened the door and got out while Sunil did the same, keeping John covered with the gun. This far from the city, there wasn't a sound, the night still and clear, the air cool and calm. John felt calm as well. Everything he had done until now had brought him to this point. He was ready. Taking a deep breath, he walked around to the house, its shape taking form in front of him now his eyes had adjusted to the darkness.

A rough gravel driveway lead into a double carport attached to the side of the large two-story villa. It was unpainted, and the windows had yet to be glazed. John turned and looked back at Sunil, and with a jerk of the gun, Sunil indicated that he should go inside. John walked up the drive and climbed the steps to the left which led to the front door. He pushed aside the large plywood sheet which was serving as a temporary door and stepped inside. He paused, allowing his eyes to adjust to the level of darkness. The air was musty, and his nose itched with the smell of cement dust. Soft moonlight fell onto a curving stairway from a skylight high above in the double height entrance hall while to the left, a door opened onto the rest of the house. Sunil stepped in beside him, jabbing his gun into John's back with his right hand. With his left hand, he pulled out his cell phone and thumbing across the screen turned on the phone's flashlight and shone the light around the hallway.

"In there on the left," he told John, nudging him in the back with the gun barrel. John turned and walked across the bare concrete floor, entering the living room which stretched the full width of the house. Broad picture windows opened onto the front garden, and to the rear, a door led to what would be the kitchen. The floor was still rough concrete, not yet tiled, and in the center of the room was a pile of rubble and builder's waste. In the far corner stood a blue plastic chair, a pile of empty plastic water bottles scattered at its feet.

"Get the chair. Sit in it," instructed Sunil from the doorway.

John walked over to the chair and picked it up. He looked around the room, scanning it carefully in the light thrown out by Sunil's phone. He needed to find an advantage, to gain the upper hand. He didn't want to die here. He walked toward the pile of rubble in the middle of the room, perhaps he could find a weapon there.

"What are you doing? Sit the fuck down."

"Yes, yes," John placed the chair next to the rubble pile, turned it to face Sunil and sat down. Sunil turned off his phone flashlight, waited for his eyes to adjust, then walked into the room. He circled the room, John's eyes following him. He walked behind John and at the last-minute, John sensed a movement of air, a shifting of electrons, something. He flinched, but it didn't help as the barrel of the gun smashed against the side of his head, knocking him to the floor. He lay there stunned, pain radiating through his skull, his eyes filled with spots of light. The toe of Sunil's boot connected hard with his shoulder and he grunted in pain.

"Get up, you foreign fuck."

John picked himself up from the floor, righting the chair. In the dim light, he spied a piece of steel piping lying on the edge of the rubble pile. As he sat down, he nudged the pipe closer to the chair with his foot. It might come in useful later. The side of his head throbbed, and he pressed his hand to it, feeling a sticky liquid beneath his fingertips. It took him a moment to realize it was blood.

Sunil stood over him, breathing fast and heavy, the gun in his right hand hanging at his side, his finger still curled around the trigger.

"You think you are better than me, you foreign piece of shit. Huh? Do you even know who you are dealing with? You think you can push me around? I am Sunil Patil. My father is Surya Patil. We rule this city."

John took a deep breath. Time to go on the offensive. He craned his head back to look Sunil in the eye.

"You? Rule this city?" he scoffed. "You are just a jumped-up little shit, living off your parent's money. You still live at home! What have you ever done in life? Even your so-called great father is robbing the country blind."

"Shut the fuck up!"

John ignored him and continued, "You are driving around in a Mercedes. How did your dad pay for that on a government salary? What about the house you live in? How many millions of rupees did it cost? You hypocrites have perfected the art of robbing your own people, and you think you are great."

Sunil breathed faster, his chest heaving, eyes wild. "You don't come here and tell me what to do. My father is a businessman. All his money is because of his skill at business. We deserve everything we have."

John sneered, then forced a laugh. "Bullshit. You don't give a fuck about anyone other than yourself. Your father cheats the public, and you are a useless, good-for-nothing loser who lives with his parents, spends all their money because you are too useless to do anything yourself. You and all your friends are losers."

Sunil roared with anger and stepped forward, raising his gun in the air to pistol-whip John in the head. John threw himself to the floor and reached for the steel pipe with his right hand, swinging it hard at the side of Sunil's knee. He heard a satisfying crack, and Sunil howled in pain. His finger tightened on the trigger in reflex, and a gunshot echoed around the room, the sound deafening them both. His legs buckled beneath him and he sank to the floor, his face screwed up in pain and fury. He twisted around and brought the gun to bear on John. John rolled out of the way and swung the pipe again this time connecting with Sunil's wrist. Sunil shrieked, and the gun fell from his now useless fingers. John swung his leg around and kicked the gun across the floor away from his reach. Sunil grabbed at John's leg with his left hand, but John twisted out of the way. He jumped to his feet and stepped back from Sunil's grasp as he crawled toward him. John stepped to the side and kicked Sunil hard on his wounded knee. Sunil collapsed on the floor, retching with the pain.

John walked over and picked up the gun, then walked back to Sunil. He kicked him in the knee again, causing Sunil to cry out in pain.

"I've waited a long time to do this, you fucking bastard." John spat on Sunil's face. "You think you can run around doing whatever you want, to whoever you want. Well, that ends today." John stood on Sunil's injured wrist, gradually increasing the pressure.

"Stop, stop, please. I'll give you money, anything," Sunil sobbed.

John squatted down beside him.

"You think I'm doing this for money? You think that's the most important thing to me? I'm not like you. You are the scum of the earth. You took something extremely precious from me. Someone who meant everything to me. No amount of money will ever bring her back."

"I'm sorry, I'm sorry. It was a mistake. The others made me do it."

"Really? You expect me to believe that? The others wouldn't move unless you said so. I know, I've watched you for weeks, followed you. I know everything about you. You are a bully, living off your dad's power and influence. And look at you now, lying there sniveling like a little baby. Where's your dad now? Where's all your money now?"

"Please don't kill me, please don't kill me, I'm sorry," Sunil whimpered.

John stood, looking down at Sunil in disgust. He contemplated shooting him in the other kneecap, making him suffer more, but he wanted to finish it. John had had enough. It was over now.

He stepped back, took a deep breath.

"This is for you, Charlotte."

Raising the gun, he shot Sunil in the head.

It took a few minutes for the ringing in John's ears to stop. He used the time to remove all traces of him being there. With a rag he had found in another room, he wiped his fingerprints off the chair and the pipe, before hiding the pipe in the rubble pile and covering it with sand.

After wiping the gun, he carefully positioned it in Sunil's hand, making sure his finger was around the trigger.

He took one last look around the room, making sure he had left no trace, then walked out the front door. On the top step, he paused and listened. The only sound was the chirping of crickets in the fields behind the villa, the only movement the twinkling of the billions of stars overhead. John exhaled and smiled. Time to go home.

John had three days before his flight was to depart, and he used the time wisely. It didn't take long to reattach the fuse for the GPS tracker in the rental car, then he washed the vehicle thoroughly and wiped down the interior before giving it a good vacuum.

He deleted the search history on his phone and laptop and removed the SIM card from the phone. He backed up his laptop to the cloud, then took the phone and the laptop out into the back garden where he smashed them both to pieces with a hammer. After dropping off the hire car, he drove around the town in the Scorpio, dropping pieces of phone and laptop in various rubbish heaps. Back at home, he examined himself in the mirror. He didn't look too bad. The cut on his head was hidden by his hair, and the bruising on his body was hidden by his clothing.

It was only the evening of the next day when news reports appeared on the local TV channels that a body had been found in a building site on the outskirts of the city. An apparent suicide. Over the following day, the reports became more detailed, the reporters excitedly mentioning the body was, in fact, that of Sunil Patil, son of Progressive People's Alliance Party leader, Surya Patil. Reporters besieged the politician's Shivnagar house, questioning anyone who came in or out of the building.

Mr. Patil himself was unavailable for comment, but reports leaked from the household of Sunil's battles with alcoholism and his fight with depression after the recent deaths of his friends. Messages of sympathy came from political leaders in Delhi, and the leaders of the opposing political parties were quick to grab screen time, expressing sympathy but also unable to resist a dig at their opponent, wondering how his son was in possession of an unlicensed weapon.

Two days later, however, the news was filled with juicier headlines, some scandal or other involving government contracts in another part of India, replacing any speculation about Sunil's death.

John watched it all with no small amount of amusement, relieved nothing had been linked back to him. The movers came and packed up the house, and he handed the keys back to the landlord. He sold his car to a dealer for less than its market value, happy he could offload it quickly. He spent his last night in the city at his favorite Hotel, The Oberoi, where he enjoyed a relaxing evening, sipping gin and tonics on the beautifully manicured lawn of the Polo Club Bar.

British Airways flight BA118 to London departed at seven a.m., and despite the early hour, John was there well in advance. He was keen to leave. There was nothing left for him in Bangalore, and he had no desire to linger or even return. Until Charlotte's death, it had been a wonderful posting. He had made a lot of good friends but had shut himself off from all of them once Charlotte died. It was time to move on and start a new life somewhere else.

The hotel car pulled over in the drop-off lane at the airport, and he got out, the chauffeur helping him with his bags and bidding him farewell with a smile. John shook his hand, slipping him a hundred-rupee note, and turned toward the terminal. He wheeled his bag along the path before crossing the separate VIP Lane separating the public drop-off area from the terminal.

John heard his name being called and turned to his left to see a white police Bolero parked at the curb, the slim figure of Inspector Rajiv leaning against the hood. John's heart skipped a beat, but he forced himself to remain calm and walked over as Rajiv straightened up and smiled.

"Mr. Hayes. John." Rajiv extended his hand.

"Inspector. Rajiv." John smiled nervously.

"So, you are leaving our fine city?"

"Yes, I fly out in a couple of hours. What brings you here at such an early hour?"

Rajiv smiled. "I wanted to say goodbye. I thought you would leave soon, but I couldn't reach you on your phone, so I called in a few favors with the ticketing office to find out when." He grinned, "Being a policeman has its advantages."

John smiled and nodded.

"I'm sorry your experience was not a happy one. Perhaps if things had been different, you could have made a home for yourself here."

"Yes, who knows how things could have been?"

Rajiv studied John's face. "Do you think you will ever come back?"

"I doubt it Rajiv. I doubt it very much."

Rajiv nodded and looked away, his eyes flicking over the people arriving at the airport. "It's probably better you don't come back." He looked at John again. "I suppose you heard the news about Sunil Patil?"

"Yes, I saw it on TV. That was unfortunate. He must have been very depressed."

"Yes, apparently so." Rajiv looked down at his feet before looking up again and fixing John in his gaze. "Unusually too, he had a shattered kneecap and a broken wrist."

John raised his eyebrows, "Really?"

"Hmmm. It's strange. But I believe he tripped in the dark and injured himself. He did have a lot of alcohol in his system."

John nodded cautiously.

"It must have been quite difficult though for him to shoot himself with his broken wrist, and we still haven't worked out how he got there." Rajiv smiled, "But I don't want to trouble you with a conversation like this before your flight. I guess it's one of those mysteries that will never get solved." He extended his hand again. "You have a safe flight, John. Who knows, maybe our paths will cross again in the future?"

John shook his hand. "You are a good man Inspector Rajiv Sampath. A good man. Maybe it's time you did something more fulfilling."

"Maybe you are right, John. Maybe you are right."

EPILOGUE

Pournima heard a knock on the door. She dried her hands on her *dupatta* and pushed aside the curtain separating the tiny kitchen from the living room. She glanced into the bedroom where little Geetanjali lay sleeping on a blanket on the floor before moving to the front door. She didn't get many visitors these days. There had been a lot at first when Sanjay was killed, the neighbors rallying around and bringing food and offering support. But that could only last so long, people needed to get on with their own lives, and now she was pretty much left to her own devices. Life was tough as a single mother, and without Sanjay's income, Pournima was struggling to make ends meet. She was earning a small wage cleaning for a family in one of the fancy apartment blocks, but that money could only go so far, and she wasn't even sure how she would pay the next month's school fees for Saumya.

She unlatched the door, opened it slightly, and peered out. She stiffened when she saw a police officer standing outside on the road. Pournima remembered him, he was the one who had questioned Sanjay at the hospital all those months ago. He had been pleasant then, but she had an inbuilt mistrust of the police. You never knew which ones you could trust, and she didn't know if she could trust this one.

"Pournima, ma'am?"

"Yes," Pournima kept the door only slightly open.

"I was asked to give this to you, ma'am, by a friend of mine." He held out a large brown envelope. "He thought you might find the contents useful." She looked at it nervously, then curiosity getting the better of her, opened the door wider and took the envelope.

"Is everything okay, ma'am?"

She nodded.

"Your daughters?"

"Yes, okay." She wondered how he knew about her daughters.

"Ma'am, if you ever need anything, if there is ever any trouble, please give me a call." He handed her a card. "You can call me anytime. My mobile number is on the card."

"Thank you." Pournima nodded, noticing Padma watching nosily from the door of her house across the road. No doubt she would be the next person to knock on the door.

The policeman nodded and turned to walk back to his car. She watched him go, then closed the door and looked down at the name on the card in her hand. Inspector Rajiv Sampath. With a pin, she stuck the card to the door frame beside the kitchen, then looked at the envelope. It was bulky and surprisingly heavy. She stuck the tip of her thumb under the flap and ripped it open. Inside were three large packages wrapped in newspaper and a single slip of paper. She reached in and pulled out one of the packages. She placed the envelope on the floor and tore off the newspaper.

"*Devare,*" she gasped. Inside the newspaper was a brick-sized bundle of two thousand rupee notes bound together with a rubber band. Pournima dropped the bundle on the floor and reached for the others. They were the same. It was more money than she had ever seen in her life. She threw the bundles into the air and jumped up and down for joy. The noise woke Geetanjali who sat up from her bed and rubbed her eyes. Pournima couldn't believe it. All her money worries were over. She pulled the single piece of paper from the envelope and unfolded it. Pournima didn't understand much English, but she recognized the three words written on the paper. Her lips moved silently, sounding out the words as she traced over them with her finger, *For the girls.*

GLOSSARY

- **Aarti** - a Hindu religious ritual of worship, a part of puja, in which light from wicks soaked in ghee (purified butter) or camphor is offered to one or more deities.
- **Devare** - My God (Kannada Language)
- **Devi Ashirvada** - A religious greeting in Kannada the language of the Indian State of Karnataka, that means "blessings of the Goddess.
- **Dhaba** - A roadside eatery or cafe
- **Dupatta** - A scarf/shawl originally worn by women as a symbol of modesty but now considered an integral part of traditional women's clothing.
- **Hey Bhagwan** - Oh my God!
- **Kurta** - A long loose fitting cotton shirt worn by men and often paired with loose fitting cotton pants called pyjama.
- **Panditji** - Priest
- **Pooja** - A prayer ritual/ceremony

- **Tilaka** - A religious mark made on a Hindu's forehead as a sign of piety or religious affiliation. Often made from sandalwood paste, ash, or in this story's instance red vermillion

JOIN MY NEWSLETTER

The next book is currently being written, but if you sign up for my VIP newsletter I will let you know as soon as the next book is released.

By signing up for the newsletter you will also receive advanced discounted links to all new-releases.

Your email will be kept 100% private and you can unsubscribe at any time.

If you are interested, please visit my website

www.markdavidabbott.com
(No Spam. Ever.)

ACKNOWLEDGMENTS

I would like to thank the following without whose support this book wouldn't have been possible.

My wife K, for encouraging me to continue writing and who frequently dragged me out from the pit of self doubt. My editor Sandy Ebel - Personal Touch Editing whose advice and input has made me "rite proppa", and Angie-O e-Covers for a rocking cover. I would also like to thank Mr. Ramesh for his invaluable input regarding the structure of the Indian Police Force as well as technical advice regarding weapons.

ABOUT THE AUTHOR

Mark can be found online at:
www.markdavidabbott.com

on Facebook
www.facebook.com/markdavidabbottauthor

or on email at: www.markdavidabbott.com/contact

Printed in Great Britain
by Amazon